POINT MAN

BROTHERS COURAGEOUS, BOOK 4

VANESSA GRAY BARTAL

DRY CREEK PRESS

Copyright © 2012, 2021 Vanessa Gray Bartal

❀ Created with Vellum

*T*ravis Vega left the recruiter's office, a smug smile of satisfaction on his face. Enlisting had felt every bit as good as he thought it might. He was on a natural high, which was good because he was still too young to stop in a bar and get drunk. There was one thing he could legally do now, something he had been longing for since he was fourteen.

He detoured away from his car and headed down a darker, dingier street. There was no one behind the desk when he walked inside the dilapidated building, but Travis wasn't surprised—tattoo parlors weren't the type of place where one usually found a receptionist.

"Yo," he called.

"In a minute," a surly voice replied from a darkened back room. Travis drummed his fingers on the counter, scanning the rows of pictures while he waited his turn.

"See anything you like?" a man said as he bowed through the doorway and wiped his massive hands on a rag. Travis hoped it was a good sign the guy actually used soap and water to wash them.

"I don't need to look; I know what I want," Travis said, his voice dripping with satisfaction.

"Let's go," huge, hand-wiping guy said, bobbing his head toward the back room.

Travis followed, searching himself for any signs of fear. Not that he would allow fear to deter him, because he wouldn't. But, either way, he didn't find a trace of nerves.

"Whad'ya want, kid?" Burly guy spoke as one meaty paw shoved Travis into a chair.

"I'm eighteen," Travis said, ready to reach for his wallet to prove his age.

"Yippee for you, now what do you want?" he enunciated the words in case Travis might have misunderstood. At any other time, Travis might have taken exception with his presumptuously rude attitude, but not now. Now Travis loved it because it fit with everything he had ever thought about getting a tattoo. If he had entered and the guy had been quietly sipping tea while reading the *Wall Street Journal*, then Travis would have run away screaming.

"I want a hog," Travis said. "There." He lifted his sleeve to indicate the spot on his bicep. "A wild boar with long tusks. Think you can handle it?"

The guy didn't reply. Instead he picked up a sketch pad and pen and drew a picture. He finished and handed the notepad to Travis. There was a little part of him, the part that remained an anime-loving dork, who recognized that the guy had real talent. But the punk kid part of him wouldn't deign to admit it. "That'll do," he said. "Just don't mess it up on my arm."

The big guy didn't reply, but he got his revenge in another way because the tattoo hurt, much more than Travis thought it should. But when it was finished, it was perfect. "Awesome," Travis said with some of his old enthusiasm. Then he remembered that he was no longer an impressionable happy-go-lucky kid, and he cleared his throat. "I guess," he added begrudgingly. He paid the man and walked back to his car, a happy spring in his step that belied the thug image he was trying to promote.

He experienced his first taste of nerves as soon as he parked outside his house, a house that would be his no longer. A little bit of grief invaded at that thought, but Travis blocked it out. Today wasn't the day for regret; today was the day for vengeance.

His father was in his study when Travis walked through the door.

"Trav, come here a minute," his dad said. For the first time in forever, there was no command in his tone. In spite of the imperative phrase, the tone had been almost a question, as if Travis actually had some choice in the matter. An ounce of regret tried to intrude on his good mood, but he tamped it down and banished it before it could take root, slouching to his father's study as slowly as humanly possible.

"Yeah?"

His father gave him the look, and Travis straightened despite his best intentions.

"Yes, sir?" Travis amended, hating himself for giving in.

His father smiled as if there had been no altercation and picked up the letter from his desk. "It came."

Travis suppressed his smile. This was the moment he had been waiting for. "What came?" he feigned innocence.

His father made no attempt to hide his exasperation. "Your letter from the Naval Academy."

"What if I didn't get in?" Travis goaded.

"Don't be stupid," his father said. And it was a stupid question; the son of a four-star admiral would get in the Naval Academy or die trying. "Open it." The commanding tone was back, and Travis almost felt relieved. It would be so much more fun to deliver his bombshell news to the father he was used to instead of one who was pretending to be nice.

He reached for the letter slowly, making his father impatiently hold it in his hand for the maximum length of time. He opened it with great care, but his father didn't mind that. In his mind, the old man probably thought Travis was trying not to rip it so he could save it forever as one of his most valuable treasures. Finally, the seal was perfectly broken and Travis slowly withdrew the letter, reading each word to himself while his father jittered impatiently, which was something else to enjoy. Caldwell Vega was not a man who jittered.

At last he finished the letter and folded it, sticking it gently back into the envelope.

"Well?" Caldwell bellowed. "What did it say?"

"It said I was accepted," Travis said.

Caldwell sank back into his cushy leather chair with a sigh of relief, as if he had actually been concerned Travis might not have made it. After the initial relief was over, he beamed. "Excellent. Congratulations, son."

Travis smiled, too, but if his father knew him at all, he would have been worried by that smile. "Too bad I can't go," Travis said, as softly and smoothly as he had always dreamed.

Caldwell froze. "What do you mean you can't go?" he asked, his voice falling to a silky whisper that had quelled countless sailors under his command.

"Well, you see, Dad, I made other plans."

Caldwell sat back, templing his fingers under his chin. "I already told you your stupid band is finished, Travis. It's time to grow up and take responsibility for your life."

"I couldn't agree more, sir," Travis said, the picture of son-like humility. "Which is why I did exactly that." Then, never breaking eye contact with his father, he rolled up his sleeve and showed his father his new tattoo.

For a few priceless seconds, Caldwell merely stared at it, trying to pretend it wasn't what he thought it was. And then he exploded. "You mean to tell me you enlisted in the marines?" he bellowed, springing up from behind his desk so Travis had to force himself not to cower. His father was an admittedly scary man, but this was his moment. When he had dreamed of this moment, he had happily broken into the Marine Hymn. Now he simply nodded and tried not to quiver.

"Let me see if I understand this," Caldwell said, his voice returning to the silky whisper that was somehow more terrifying than the yelling. "Your father is a four star admiral in the navy. Your brother is a naval officer, your grandfather was a naval captain during Vietnam, your great grandfather was a naval commander during World War II, and you are throwing away an officer's career in the proudest branch of the armed forces so you can be an enlisted jarhead?"

"That sounds about right," Travis said, regaining some of his earlier cockiness. The outlandish surprise had felt as good as he thought it might.

Caldwell stared at him for another minute, and Travis could see the cold calculation taking place in his eyes. "Get out," he said at last.

"Yes, sir," Travis said, managing a small salute. After all, his father was a senior officer now.

"I don't mean get out of my office," Caldwell said. "I mean get out of my house."

If he thought this would be a surprise, then he was sadly mistaken. Travis smiled because he had been correct. "My bags are already packed," he said. He turned around and left the house, never looking back.

CHAPTER 1

Kelsey woke with the feeling someone was watching him. He jumped, ready to lunge for his gun, when he realized he was home and not on assignment. Someone *was* watching him, however.

Ashton sat beside his bed, an open ring box exposing a brilliant diamond.

"This is so sudden but, yes," Kelsey said. "A thousand times yes, of course I'll marry you."

Ashton snapped the box closed and stood. "I don't know why I thought it was a good idea to come to you for advice. I'm calling Nick."

"Wait," Kelsey said, swiping his hand over his face a few times to try and wake up. "What's the deal?"

Ashton sat back down. "I'm nervous."

"Because you think proposing to your girlfriend at this stage in your life is the biggest mistake you've ever made?" Kelsey guessed.

Ashton blinked at him, stoic. "Seriously, why am I talking to you?"

"Okay, apparently that's not why. Why don't you tell me instead of making me guess?"

"I don't know how to do it. I see these guys on TV and they're always making grand gestures. When I do it, I want it to be memorable and awesome for Shelby, but I don't know what I'm doing. I'm not of the grand gesture variety."

Kelsey stretched out his arms and popped his knuckles. "You came to the right marine. I may not know anything about relationships, loyalty, commitment, marriage, honor, devotion, maturity, or longevity, but I am the king of grand gestures. How does Shelby feel about JumboTrons?"

Ashton groaned and pulled out his phone, no doubt dialing Nick.

"I was kidding. It's like you have no sense of humor anymore," Kelsey complained.

"Not when it comes to this," Ashton said. "I'm serious about this. I want to do it right."

"All right, no JumboTrons," Kelsey said.

"Shelby would hate that," Ashton said. "She wouldn't want to be a public spectacle."

"That rules out most of my best ideas, but have no fear; we'll think of something." Noting Ashton's still-dismal expression, he added, "I'm serious; we'll think of something. I actually am sort of gifted at this stuff. We'll find something suited for Shelby."

"It's not that. It's this whole day; it's depressing." Ashton sighed heavily, the sound echoing what Kelsey felt.

"So you're not of the camp that thinks Travis and Caleigh are making a lifelong love match today?" Kelsey asked.

"Is anyone in that camp?"

"Caleigh," Kelsey replied. They were quiet for a minute, each pitying Caleigh because she had no idea what her future held, but they did. They had lived with Travis the last few months. Caleigh saw what she wanted in their newest team member, but it wasn't the truth.

"I feel like the guy standing on the deck of the Titanic shouting, 'Iceberg,' and no one is listening," Kelsey added.

"I feel like we're offering up Caleigh on the sacrificial pyre of military honor," Ashton said. "Whose idea was this marriage anyway?"

"Travis's dad," Kelsey said.

"The Admiral?" Ashton asked. As always, he was the last to know everything.

"The Admiral," Kelsey said. "Apparently he's threatening that either Travis make good and marry her or he'll press for a court martial."

"Can he do that?" Ashton asked.

"Uniform Code of Military Justice Article One Thirty Four—so vague it should scare the pants off every man intent on having fun."

"Good thing I've changed my definition of fun," Ashton mused.

Kelsey didn't reply since he was now in the minority among his married or soon-to-be-married friends.

"Are you taking Melly to the wedding?" Ashton asked.

"You have got to spend more time on Instagram, Dude. You're so far out of the loop. No, I'm taking someone else. And Nick said that Ashleigh said that Melly said she's not taking a date."

"Your life is sad," Ashton said in his deadpan way of blurting factual information.

"My life is fine," Kelsey said. "And wait until you see my date. Smoking hot. I met her at my veterinarian's office."

"Why do you have a veterinarian when you don't have a dog yet?" Ashton asked.

"I'm pre-screening vets, duh. Not anyone can treat my precious pet, whenever I eventually get one," Kelsey said.

"When you started thinking about getting a dog, you realized you had never tried to pick up a woman at a vet's office, huh?" Ashton guessed.

Kelsey leaned forward and spoke earnestly. "You have no idea how many hot women own animals. You know when you go to the gym to work out how it's testosterone overload and every woman who walks in the door is suddenly attractive? The vet's office is like that in reverse; it's the place to go for estrogen overload. I'm convinced if I had a snaggletooth and peg leg I could still pick someone up there. I feel like planting a flag for this discovery."

"Your life is sad," Ashton repeated.

"My life is exactly what I want it to be," Kelsey said, somewhat defensively because Ashton had hit a nerve. So maybe he had been a little lonely the last few weeks since he and Melly arrived home from California. And maybe he felt a little bored and restless. There was also the distinct possibility he had actually locked himself in his room one night with a sad movie and a pint of ice cream while he wallowed in Melly's refusal to move in with him. Big deal. He was better now. Things were back on track.

"If you say so," Ashton said. He stood again and tucked the ring back in his pocket.

"What's the timeframe on the proposal?" Kelsey asked. He intended to do some serious thinking on Ashton's behalf, sure he could come up with something spectacular.

"As soon as possible after we stop mourning the loss of Caleigh's innocence," Ashton said. He let himself out of Kelsey's room

Kelsey lay back, scowling at the ceiling. The mention of Caleigh and Travis and their upcoming nuptials had left a bad taste in his mouth that wouldn't go away anytime soon. He wished there was some way to stop the approaching train wreck. Did anyone think this marriage was a good idea?

THERE WAS ONE PERSON. Caleigh Desmond stared at herself in the full length mirror, full of rainbows and sunshine when she thought of her future. She was getting married, and she was having a baby. The order hadn't come the way she wished, and she felt bad about that. But not bad enough to cloud this day. She wasn't showing yet, so she wouldn't have to wear her shame on her sleeve. People would know, but they wouldn't say anything, so she could simply relax and enjoy this day— the best day of her life.

Her reflection turned dreamy as she began to plot her future. She would cook for Travis every day he was home, and she would make big welcome home meals for him like Ashleigh did for Nick. Travis didn't know it, but Caleigh was a very good cook, like her mother and sister. There were a lot of things he didn't know about her, good things, and she was excited to show him. She would be a good wife and mother, she was sure. Wasn't this what she had been training for her whole life? Unlike Ashleigh, Caleigh had never wanted a career. She had only ever wanted marriage and a family, and now she was going to get it, a little earlier than she expected, but that was a good thing, right? She and Travis would be young parents and that meant they would still be young after their kids left the home. They could spend their golden years unfettered, traveling the country together. Maybe they would buy a Winnebago.

Of course, that was a far-off dream. For now things would be tight, but that was okay. Caleigh had never been extravagant. She had a good head on her shoulders, even when it came to finances. She was sure she could live frugally within whatever Travis made so she didn't have to work. More than anything she wanted to be a stay-at-home mom.

They would have more kids. Travis had never said how many kids he wanted, but everyone loved kids, didn't they? Caleigh wanted four, but if Travis didn't want that many, she was willing to compromise on three. Their home would be open, welcoming and cozy, like the home she had grown up in. She would be the mom who befriended her kids' friends, taking them in and making them a part of the family.

Her parents entered her room without knocking, reluctantly pulling Caleigh from her happy daydreams. "Hi," she said, her bright tone a sharp contrast to their drawn features. If there was one thing she felt truly bad about, it was that her actions had hurt her parents. She loved her parents; she hadn't meant to rebel against them or break their hearts. Things with Travis snowballed out of control. She hadn't even realized what happened until after it was over. Who knew she could get pregnant her first time? Not her. And Travis hadn't realized she wasn't on the pill, hadn't quite believed her when she said she was a virgin. Or maybe he had. There had been a sort of challenging gleam in his eyes since they met, one that told her she was an obstacle to be conquered. She frowned, not liking that analogy. No, she was a prize to be won, and he had won her, like knights of old jousting for their maidens. Yes, that was better.

"Caleigh, it's not too late to undo this," her father said with no preamble. He took her hands in his and gave her a grave look. "We can call off this wedding right now."

Caleigh fought a wave of impatience that was new to her. She had never felt irritated with her parents before this ordeal. Maybe it was the hormones. "Dad, I don't want to call off the wedding. I love Travis. I want to get married. And I don't get it—I thought you guys were all for getting married when you're pregnant."

"In a perfect world yes, Caleigh," he said. "But this isn't a perfect world, and this isn't a good situation. Travis is..." he bit back what he wanted to say, not wanting to alienate her further. "He has some issues, honey. I don't want his baggage to become yours, to harm you."

Caleigh laughed and hugged her father tightly. "Oh, Dad, that's not going to happen. I know he has some issues, but they're not going to affect me. I'm me, and I always will be. I can help him. I can fix him."

Instead of replying, her father hugged her tightly and pressed his face to her hair, weeping. Caleigh was shaken. She had never seen her father cry like this. She had no idea what to do, so she burst into tears, too.

"Caleigh, please understand marriage doesn't work that way," her mother said through her own tears. "You can't fix someone, honey. You go into the marriage with what you have and it can either work for you or against you. Travis needs more help than you can give him. This is not going to go well; you're not going to be happy. Please, please reconsider."

The irritation flared to life again. "Mom, Travis will get court martialed if I don't marry him. He could get thrown out of the marines and go to *jail*," Caleigh said. She was angry at her soon-to-be father-in-law. He was so mean to Travis.

"Honey, that was Admiral Vega's way of trying to get Travis to do the right thing. But if you're the one who backs out, then he'll be free and clear."

"I don't want to back out," Caleigh said. She wanted to stomp her foot in impatience, but her father was still clinging to her as he tried to get his emotions under control, so she couldn't. "I'm happy. Why can't you guys see this is a good thing?"

Her mother stared at her with sad eyes. "Oh, Caleigh, I wish I could impart my wisdom to you in a way you would believe and understand."

Caleigh resisted the urge to roll her eyes, not wanting to be disrespectful to them when they were struggling so much. *They* were the ones who didn't understand. Couldn't they see how happy she was? How very perfect her life was right now? This was the right thing to do, and Caleigh was confused about why she was the only one who saw it that way. Even Travis had rebelled at the idea of getting married, though Caleigh thought he was actually rebelling against his father. Admiral Vega was used to ordering people's lives for them, and Travis had never liked that, had never allowed it. Now at last he had a chance to do it using military channels, and there was nothing Travis could do about it. That was why Travis was upset, not because of her or the baby. He loved her; she was sure of it.

Her parents finally pulled themselves together and left the room. Caleigh was glad to see them go, and that gladness made her feel guilty. She loved her parents and knew they only wanted the best for her. Why couldn't they comprehend that this was what was best? She was baffled by their reaction.

Her sister, Ashleigh, entered almost as soon as her parents left. Caleigh scrunched her face into a defensive pout and squared off against her big sister. They had never argued before. Ashleigh had always been a nurturer, and Caleigh had always been adoring. But today Caleigh wasn't in the mood for more lectures.

"Don't start, Ashleigh. I already got it from Mom and Dad, and I don't want to hear it from you. If you can't be happy for me, then go back out. I'm trying to have a good day here, and I don't want people ruining it with sad faces."

Ashleigh froze, taken aback by her little sister's unorthodox outburst. Then she smiled, came forward, and wrapped Caleigh in a tight hug. "I love you, and you look amazing. I was simply coming to tell you if you need anything at all, ever, I am here for you. Always. Nick, too. We think you're the greatest, and you're about the most beautiful bride on the planet." She leaned in and kissed Caleigh's cheeks with a dazzling blitz of kisses that made Caleigh's earlier irritation fade into a round of heartfelt giggles.

"I'm so happy, Ashleigh," Caleigh said. Ashleigh didn't reply, but she clung a little tighter, and when she let her go, her eyes were moist with unshed tears.

Ashleigh left, and Caleigh stared at the mirror again, taking up her daydreams where she had left off.

CHAPTER 2

Unlike Caleigh, Travis was not thinking about his bride, upcoming wedding, or future. Instead, he was thinking about his father and resenting the fact that his father had beaten him at his own game. How had he allowed the military to be used against him? He had not seen that coming. When Caleigh told him she was pregnant, he had felt an odd combination of fear and excitement. Having a kid might actually be fun, though having his wages garnished for child support would not. But he had been willing to do his duty and pay up. He had even been willing to do the dad thing whenever he was stateside. He foresaw his relationship with Caleigh continuing for a while. She was sweet and beautiful. He had never pictured himself with someone so innocent, but he found he rather enjoyed her innocence. It made him feel good in a way he couldn't put his finger on. She was also pleasant and pliable, never demanding more from him than he was willing to give.

Then his father found out about the baby, and everything went downhill from there. He had pressured Travis to, "Be a man and do the right thing," whatever that meant. Travis had assured him he was willing to pay child support, but, as always, that wasn't good enough for his father. He demanded Travis step up and propose. Travis had actually laughed at that.

"I'm twenty three, Admiral. I'm not getting married."

"If you're old enough to get a girl pregnant, then you're old enough to take responsibility for your actions and make things right," Caldwell had responded.

Travis had laughed again, secure in the knowledge his father's talk was all bluster and he wasn't in any danger. And then his father had pulled the ace out of his sleeve.

"Marry the girl, or you're out of the marines," Caldwell had said, going on to explain the archaic and vague law that could find him liable for immoral conduct unbecoming a soldier. Travis knew better than to think he was bluffing; Caldwell had enough clout to press the matter. For a while, Travis had considered quitting, dropping out of his career to deny his father the satisfaction of winning—again. But he liked the marines. He liked being a part of his new team, much more than they liked him at the moment, but still. He wasn't ready to give up what he had worked for the last five years to squelch his father's indomitable control. So he had given in.

He bought Caleigh a tiny diamond, wincing at the ding in his finances, and even managed to do the proposal up right by taking her to dinner and getting down on one knee. Caleigh had cried and, for one brief moment, he had felt happy, as if maybe he actually was doing the right thing. Then things had snowballed and now, two weeks later, he was going to be a married man. That fact didn't bother him nearly as much as his father's victory, though. There had to be some way to get back at the old man, didn't there? Travis was sure if he thought hard enough, he could find it.

"Nervous?" his too-perfect big brother, Gage, asked. Of course Gage would be by his side lending support because Gage always, always did the right thing. Despite the fact that Gage and their father were two peas in a pod, Travis had never resented him. Caleigh and he had this one thing in common, at least—they had both been lucky in the older sibling department. Gage had been as good a big brother as he had been at everything else in his life, meaning he was perfect in that area, too.

Travis shrugged. "A little, I guess."

"She seems like a sweet girl. The family is nice," Gage noted.

"If you like that sort," Travis said.

Gage laughed. "What sort? The incredibly loving, well-adjusted, and supportive type?"

"Yeah, that type. But they're also interfering, you know?" It was Reverend Desmond who had called his father to confer, not realizing Travis and his dad hadn't spoken in three years.

"Not everyone's family is as dysfunctional as ours, Trav," Gage said. Travis was surprised to hear him admit their family had issues. As far as he knew, Gage thought their father walked on water. "This could be a good thing, Pal. Make it stick, make it work."

Travis sighed, trying and failing to feel annoyed that his brother still called him Pal like he was four years old. "I'll give it the old college try," Travis said.

"You didn't go to college," Gage pointed out.

"Then I'll give it the old high-school-graduate, barely-literate-marine-grunt try," Travis promised, grinning. His brother was one of the only people on earth who didn't rub him the wrong way because he was convinced of his genuine goodness. Gage was one of those rare people who was exactly what he purported to be—perfect in every way.

"Thatta boy," Gage said, giving him a hearty slap on the shoulder. Travis's team leader and future brother-in-law, Nick, opened the door and stepped inside. Gage gave him an assessing glance, eyeing the arms full of wicked tattoos. But then in usual Gage fashion, he glossed over the tattoos and studied Nick's face, zeroing in on his eyes. Apparently he liked what he saw because he stood and held out his hand.

"Lieutenant," Gage said. "Pleasure to meet you. Travis has told me a lot about you."

Nick smiled in a self-deprecating way that let him know he realized not all of the reports had been good. Nick and Travis had butted heads more than once the last few months. "Lieutenant," Nick returned, shaking Gage's hand. The ongoing feud between navy and marine personnel was temporarily set aside as Nick and Gage formed an instant bond. Travis had never realized before they reminded him of each other, a comparison he didn't find very comforting. He didn't want Nick to remind him of Gage; he wanted to resent him for his authority, a task made easier if he compared Nick to Caldwell instead. Now that he thought of it, though, Nick and Gage both possessed the same gentle-yet-firm leadership style, preferring to lead by example until times got tough, and then the orders started to fly. Caldwell never stopped giving orders, as far as Travis could tell.

"Ready, Private?" Nick asked, turning his attention to Travis after he and Gage finished their we're-officers-life-is-hard-at-the-top commiseration.

"Aye, sir," Travis said. He wondered if he would continue to call Nick "sir" after they were related. He called his father "sir," but that was because the old man insisted on it. Nick probably wouldn't care if they weren't on duty.

Nick studied him, probably trying to decide if he was going to give him the "So you're marrying my baby sister-in-law" talk. He had refrained so far, but he thought maybe Ashleigh had something to do with that. She seemed to be trying to convince everyone to be supportive and not add more stress to an already stressful situation. For that, Travis was thankful. He could happily live the rest of his life without any more lectures on responsibility and doing the right thing. He had heard it all his life.

"Are you married?" Nick said, turning his attention to Gage once again.

"Never had the pleasure," Gage said. Travis snickered. He was about to make a joke, something like "What's the pleasure in being manacled to one woman" when he realized he was about to be manacled in about a half hour. Suddenly the situation seemed void of humor and his smile died.

"Marriage can be the best part of life, or it can be the worst, depending on what you do with it," Nick said. He was still talking to Gage, but Travis knew the words were meant for him.

"I think things are going to turn out well," Gage said, ever the optimist.

Nick nodded, smiling as he turned and left the room. Gage shook his head as the door closed. "Knocking up your team leader's little sister-in-law. Geez, Pal, either you've got nerves of steel or you don't think about anything."

"Nerves of steel," Travis lied. Despite how many times Kelsey and Truck had tried to warn him away from Caleigh, he hadn't predicted the current outcome. He had merely thought he would have a little fun with a pretty girl and move on. But Caleigh had been as innocent as everyone said; now he was learning that innocence came with its own set of complications. For instance, everyone was so bent on protecting her they forgot his needs and desires. Last night had been his bachelor party. Gage hadn't been able to come until today, so Travis' teammates made sure he hadn't spent it at a strip club as he intended, rightly knowing Caleigh would be offended. Instead they took him to a bar with a live band. The band had been good, so it hadn't been a total bust, but he was the only one who got wasted. Even Kelsey had refrained since his shrink convinced him he was an alcoholic.

"Maybe I could quit the team," Travis said. It wasn't turning out the way he thought. He liked doing recon, enjoyed the challenge of being a point man, but the team wasn't working out and everyone knew it. He wanted buddies who understood him, who would finish a work week the way he wanted—losing themselves in a bottle of Jack together. Instead he had stumbled into a tight brotherhood of do-gooders he couldn't seem to break, no matter how hard he tried. No matter what he did, the ghost of the one who died before him was always hanging over his head. He would never admit to anyone how much it bothered him to be forever second best. He glanced at Gage; it was like being a kid all over again.

"Give it some more time, bud," Gage urged. "Too many changes at once aren't good. Settle into married life, have that baby, and then consider your options. By then maybe things will feel a little less chaotic."

Gage was undoubtedly right because Gage was always right. Never in their entire lives had he been wrong, done wrong, made one step out of line, spoken without thinking. All those things were reserved for Travis. This time, however, Travis decided to listen to his brother. It was entirely possible his desire to flee the team was actually a desire to flee his current situation. It probably wasn't much of a secret that he did not want to be married right now. He liked Caleigh well enough, but he was too young and too messed up to be anyone's idea of a husband or father. Everyone but his own father and Caleigh seemed to understand that. They were the only two people anxious for the wedding to take place.

"I suppose," Travis said. He reached into his pocket for his flask and found a note instead. "Don't even think about it," the note read, in Kelsey's handwriting, of course. He rifled through his duffle, searching for a backup, when he found another note. "Got this one, too. Man up and face it sober, Marine." He threw his bag down in disgust, giving it a kick for good measure.

"Something wrong?" Gage asked, probably knowing very well what the problem was.

"I don't suppose…" Travis let the thought trail off.

Gage shook his head. "I don't carry booze when I'm in uniform." Or ever, he could have added. That was yet another foible reserved for Travis, the family screwup. His nerves were gearing up for a massive assault. His stomach roiled the way it had the night before basic. Back then, he had spent a few hours puking into the toilet before boarding the bus that would take him to Parris Island. Swallowing hard, he dabbed at his forehead with the edge of his sleeve and tried to remember where the nearest bathroom was.

Gage rested his hands on Travis's shoulders and gave them a squeeze. "It's going to be okay, Pal. You're going to make it."

Travis looked up, biting his lip, feeling four all over again. And now, as then, he allowed his brother's words to comfort him. Despite the fact that he was a twenty-three-year-old marine, he stumbled forward and let his brother hug him fiercely, banishing the monsters as he had for as long as either of them could remember.

CHAPTER 3

*K*elsey was already regretting his choice of date. She had seemed so normal in the veterinarian's office. Maybe not normal, exactly. No woman who owned an iguana was quite normal. But he had thought her choice of pet quirky and cool. Up until about a minute ago when she dropped the bomb on him.

I sleep with Mikey.

At first Kelsey thought she was confessing the fact that she had a boyfriend, and then it registered. "Wait, isn't Mikey the name of your iguana?"

She nodded. "He gets lonely. People think iguanas are loners, but they're wrong. Iguanas are social creatures."

He refrained from telling her people didn't think iguanas were loners. People didn't think about iguanas at all, at least normal people didn't. It was time to admit to himself she had been a spite date. He wanted to show Melly he wasn't mourning her loss, so he found the first beautiful woman he could and asked her out. Now he was stuck with Chelsea-the-iguana-lady for an entire evening. To make matters worse, the sound of muffled laughter behind him told him Melly had overheard at least part of the conversation and probably knew exactly why he had asked Chelsea out. He turned to give her a freezing glare that immediately turned to heartsick longing. She looked exquisite, and her smile was dazzling.

"*Hi,*" he mouthed instead.

She winked at him and his heart turned over, like any fifteen year old seeing a pretty woman up close for the first time. He turned back around in time to catch the last part of Chelsea's statement.

"Filled with crickets. And that was when I realized iguanas are herbivores. So how was I supposed to catch the hundred crickets I had set free in my apartment?"

She paused as if actually waiting for him to answer the question. "Buy a frog?" he guessed.

"Exactly," Chelsea said, bobbing her head in enthusiastic agreement.

Kelsey wasn't sure what it said about him that he was on the same wavelength as someone who used amphibians for pest control.

"Only Mikey didn't like the first frog, so I had to get another. But crickets multiply at an alarming rate, so before I knew it I had a half dozen frogs hopping around my house. It took a while to realize Mikey was traumatized by all the frogs and crickets. I found him hiding in my underwear drawer, one of my bras wrapped around his head, and that's when I knew I had to get rid of the frogs and call an exterminator for the crickets."

Behind them, Melly chortled, ending on a snort. Kelsey knew she was making a mental joke about a perverted iguana being a bigger problem than frogs or crickets, and he had to cough to cover his own laughter. "That's, uh, rough," he said, clearing his throat. Thankfully the music started, putting an end to conversation.

Caleigh's little cousin tottered down the aisle with her basket of flowers. She was an old pro now after having performed this same maneuver only a few months ago at Ashleigh and Nick's wedding.

Ashleigh came next, a smile pasted on her face. Only those who knew her well would be able to see the sadness behind it. Kelsey thought it odd he was somehow one of those people now. However reluctantly, he had come to love this woman like a sister, and he hated to see her so upset. Everyone stood and Caleigh entered on the arm of Reverend Desmond.

What a contrast this wedding was to the last in this family. Then it had been a joyous celebration of the combination of two lives into one. Now it felt like a slow march to the guillotine. Reverend Desmond looked like the day was increasing his chances of a heart attack by about fifty percent. Only Caleigh looked radiantly happy. She beamed on everyone in attendance with her usual dose of sunshine. On any other day, it would have made those in attendance smile to see her so happy. Now it made them sad as each of them wondered if it was the last time they would see such an untroubled smile on her pretty face.

At the head of the church, Travis looked like he was about to throw up or pass out or both. He looked so bad Kelsey felt a little guilty about robbing him of his liquid courage. By now, though, he knew Travis well enough to understand he wouldn't have stopped at one sip for fortification. He would be staggering, stupid drunk, and that wasn't the kind of way for any husband of Caleigh's to come to the altar. And, if he was being honest, it felt a little too good to see Travis so miserable. They had all tried to warn him of the consequences of his rash and irresponsible behavior, had all but commanded him to stay away from Caleigh. If he was going to play the game by his own rules, then he could suck it up and take the consequences like a man.

Everyone remained dry-eyed throughout the ceremony except Reverend Desmond. Kelsey couldn't imagine what it must feel like to be a father and hand your daughter over to certain doom, but it was still disconcerting to see the usually stolid pastor so undone.

On the other side of the aisle sat Admiral Vega, in all his navy glory. He looked as imperious as a king presiding over court and Kelsey began to understand a little of Travis's rebellion. He would probably rebel, too, if he had a dad who wanted to run his life like the military ran his career. The marines were great for keeping order and discipline in the workplace, but he wouldn't want any of his former drill-sergeants for a parent. If the expression on the admiral's face was any indication, Kelsey guessed Travis's childhood hadn't been a lot of fun.

The ceremony was blessedly short, and then it was time for the reception. Caleigh's smile hadn't dimmed—if anything it was a little brighter as she flitted through the crowd, bestowing hugs on her friends and family, shaking hands with marines she hadn't yet met. Travis had managed to make a few friends closer to his own age and interests, and they were in attendance today. Kelsey had the feeling they wouldn't stick around long after they realized it was a dry reception.

Melly began shuffling toward the reception hall. Kelsey walked quickly so he could catch up and walk behind her. "Save me a dance, Mel?"

She glanced at him over her shoulder, smiling. There was no sadness in her smile, only welcome and affection, and something about that broke his heart a little. Shouldn't she be mourning his loss as much as he was mourning hers? "Sure," she said.

Chelsea Iguana, as he would henceforth think of her, shuffled up beside him. "Who's she?" she asked, her tone jealous and possessive despite the fact that this was their first date.

"My best friend," Kelsey muttered. He was kicking himself. If he hadn't done something so stupid as procuring a date for this event, then he might have had Melly to himself the whole evening. They could have danced every dance. It was doubtful she would let him kiss her, but he could have held her close. If he closed his eyes, he could imagine how she felt and smelled, but it had been too long since he felt her in his arms for real. "C'mon," he said, clasping Chelsea's hand to jet her toward the reception. It was once again his duty to present the guard for Caleigh and Travis's entrance into the reception hall. Technically it was Nick's duty since he was their commander, but Nick lacked the heart, so he begged off saying it would be weird to smack his little sister-in-law in the butt.

Kelsey lacked the heart, too, but he had no excuse other than that he *felt* like Caleigh was his little sister. Somebody had to do it, however, and he was second in command. So he gave the order and the sabers came out, creating an arch over the entering couple. He and Nick crossed swords at the end, stopping the bride and groom's progress so they could kiss.

The kiss looked real or at least affectionate, giving Kelsey a modicum of hope things might somehow turn out all right. He took a breath and swatted Caleigh across the backside. "Welcome to the marines, ma'am." His tone probably held a little too much gravity to be lighthearted, but at least he meant what he said. She was one of them now, even more than she had been before. They would do whatever was necessary to protect her, even if it meant beating the sense into her erstwhile husband. He gave the order and eight sabers clicked into place.

Chelsea was awestruck when he navigated to their table. There was a time when he would have capitalized on that and used it to get what he wanted from her. Now he was annoyed. She didn't know him, didn't know what made him tick. Why was she pretending to like him so much because he wore a uniform and carried a sword? Melly had ruined him for other women. He looked around to bestow an accusing glare and found her across the room sitting at a table with some people from the church. She looked a little sad and alone and he felt heartened, wondering if her earlier good cheer had been a front. It was pathetic how much he hoped that was the case. He was about to abandon Mikey's mom and make a dash for Melly when someone else beat him to it.

The guy who had been standing behind Travis, presumably his brother, meandered over to Melly and offered her a cup of punch. He must have said something funny because Melly laughed, and she never faked laughter. At least she never faked laughter at one of his lame jokes. Maybe she did it for strangers. He didn't think so, though, because her cheeks were coloring prettily and she invited sailor-boy to take a seat beside her.

"Where are you going?"

He hadn't realized he was heading toward Melly and her new companion until Chelsea spoke. "To get us some punch," he lied. At least the punch table was in the general direction he was headed. He could amend the lie by retrieving some on his way back.

Melly and Gilligan were deep in conversation when Kelsey arrived. "Hey," he said, a little too loudly because they both looked startled as they glanced up at him.

"Hey," Melly said, her wry tone telling him she was onto his jealousy and found it both exasperating and amusing.

"Kelsey Adams," he said, jutting his hand in the other guy's face. From his stripes, he knew he was a lieutenant, so he was already at a disadvantage.

"Gage Vega," the guy said, shaking hands. "Nice to meet you, Lance Corporal."

Was that a dig at Kelsey's lack of officer status? "Where are you stationed, sailor?" *Please say overseas.*

"Charleston," Gage said as if reading Kelsey's mind. "Only a few short hours away." He tipped his drink as if to say, *Your move, Marine.* But it was Melly who threw the next gauntlet, the traitor.

"Gage's a JAG," she said.

"A lawyer, eh?" Kelsey said. "I guess the academic pursuits are for those who couldn't make it in Special Forces."

"Then I guess those four years I spent as a SEAL were a waste of time," Gage said.

Melly propped her cheek in her hand, enjoying the spectacle. Kelsey couldn't think of anything else to say to Gage—he was an officer, a lawyer, a SEAL, nice looking, and witty. Instead he turned his attention to Melly. "You owe me a dog," he said, pointing an accusing finger at her midsection.

"Unless you expect me to go in the back room and birth a litter of puppies, I'd say that will have to wait," Melly said. Gage laughed. Kelsey wanted to punch him because he suddenly felt like the outsider.

"You agreed to a dog together. Are you going back on your word?"

"Call me tomorrow," Melly said. She glanced over his shoulder. "I think your date is stealing fruit for her iguana."

He turned and, sure enough, Chelsea was stuffing little pieces of lettuce and grapes into her purse. "Ah, criminey," he said, spinning on his heel and hurrying over before she began dismantling the centerpieces to search for edible flowers.

For the rest of the evening, he kept a sullen gaze on Melly and Gage. They danced together most of the evening, preferring the swing dances to the slow ones. Somehow that galled Kelsey even more because Melly was laughing as Gage spun her around the dance floor. *Laughing.* It was his job to make her laugh, no one else's, but this usurper was doing a good job of it if Melly's rosy cheeks and perpetual smile were any indication.

When he couldn't take the sight of them together anymore, he tore his gaze away and focused on the bride and groom. They were at the center of the room dancing, and they looked like any other bride and groom he had ever seen on their wedding day, cozy and lost in their own little world. For the second time that day, Kelsey felt a little lighter about the event. Maybe it would turn out all right after all.

TRAVIS FELT EXACTLY as he had the first time he received a concussion —dazed and sort of detached from his body. With the support of Gage, he had made it safely to the front of the church to wait for Caleigh, but then he was on his own. And he wanted to bolt. He had never been more tempted to give up everything and flee. Maybe if Gage hadn't been there, he might have tried it. But Gage would catch him. His father would drag him back, and things would be even worse. So he had stood, petrified like the world's biggest wuss while first the little cousin and then Ashleigh had walked down the aisle. Then the door opened again, and Caleigh was there.

He had heard of bridegrooms turning to mush when they caught sight of their brides, had even witnessed it when Nick married Ashleigh a few months ago. He never expected it to happen to him, especially with a girl he barely knew. But it had. Caleigh had been so radiant he was momentarily awed. He had always thought her pretty, but in her white dress and glowing from happiness, she was resplendent. Travis had dated a few girls he thought were pretty, but in the looks department, Caleigh was definitely out of their league, and his, too.

The spell was broken when she and her father reached him. The stiff and starched Reverend made no secret of his dissatisfaction in Travis—story of his life. Those in authority always had a problem with him, and the feeling was mutual. The older man's disapproval broke the spell and he was once again nauseated. Most of the ceremony was performed on autopilot, at least by him. He was glad he merely had to repeat the preacher's words because he had no idea what he was saying or doing. And then it was over.

They walked out of the church and through the arch created by his fellow marines, and the magic feeling returned. The sword ceremony would be enough to choke him up if he were he more prone to emotional displays, which he wasn't. As it was he felt a little bloom of elation. These people were here for *him*. The beautiful woman clutching his arm was now his *wife*. Whoa.

The newfound euphoria continued for the rest of the night. Even when his father clapped him on the back and smiled Travis failed to muster his usual irritation. They danced together and he felt entranced by her beauty, the ceremony, the well-wishes of their friends. It was almost an out-of-body experience. And then it was over and they were alone.

Travis's nerves returned with force as soon as they pulled away from the church. Caleigh turned behind them to wave at their friends and family, but Travis concentrated on the road. *Now what?* How badly would she freak out if he turned into a bar and got rip-roaring drunk? Even he knew that probably wasn't the best thing to do on the first night of his honeymoon, especially when his pregnant wife couldn't drink. But he was so tempted his hands twitched, yearning to turn off the highway and onto one of the seedier side streets that was destined to have alcohol.

"This was the best day," Caleigh said. She rested her hand on his leg and gave it a squeeze.

Hello. Why had he failed to consider the upside to being married?

He was heading to a hotel with a smoking hot woman who was now a sure thing. He didn't have to work for it, didn't have to get her drunk, didn't have to flatter her until she conceded. He had done that already, and now she was his. The speedometer inched up a little as his foot pressed the gas pedal. Caleigh smiled at him, her eyes twinkling as if she knew exactly what he was thinking.

They arrived at the hotel and she hovered in the background with their bags while he registered.

"Did they ask you for proof of our marriage?" Caleigh asked.

Travis laughed, thinking at first she was joking. "No, why would they?"

"I've never stayed in a hotel with anyone besides my parents before. I didn't know if that was a requirement."

He almost made the mistake of telling her he had stayed with a woman in a hotel before and that had never been procedure, but even he wasn't dumb enough to talk about other women on his honeymoon. He opened the door, dropped their bags, and reached for Caleigh. She went willingly into his arms and kissed him with far more sweetness than passion. His hands fumbled for her zipper, but she stilled them and took a step back.

"I know it's sort of silly since I'm pregnant and all, but would it be okay if we had an old-fashioned wedding night?"

He blinked at her in confusion, not sure of her meaning. For him, an old fashioned wedding night meant being too drunk to remember any of it. He glanced longingly at the mini fridge, wondering if it contained any of those ridiculously expensive miniaturized bottles of liquor.

Caleigh, sensing his confusion, hastened to explain. "I mean I want to slip into the bathroom, freshen up, change my clothes. That kind of stuff." If she was disappointed he wasn't in the same frame of mind, she didn't show it, but then Caleigh had always been sweet and unassuming.

"Sure," he said.

She smiled as she backed away, taking her luggage into the bathroom with her. As soon as the door closed between them, he hastened to the mini fridge and flung it open, cursing in exasperation when he saw it was empty. His gaze turned calculating as he studied the bathroom door. How long would she be in there? Did he have enough time to run to the store for a bottle of Jack? For that matter, shouldn't someone have sent them some champagne? It was odd to him Caleigh's family and friends didn't drink. What was the point of a wedding without a little celebration? Wasn't there some story about Jesus changing the water into wine? He would ask Caleigh's father sometime when he wanted to annoy him. So far the two had kept their distance, but that couldn't last forever. Travis sensed Reverend Desmond's disapproval and disappointment a mile away, and it made him angry. What right did the old man have to judge him when he barely knew him? So he had gotten Caleigh knocked up. He was hardly the first man in history to do so. What was the big deal? For all the pastor knew, Travis was potentially the best husband and father in the world.

He was still contemplating when the bathroom door cracked open and Caleigh peered out. Her nervousness was both endearing and annoying. True, the one time they hooked up had been so quick most of their clothes had remained on. But it was the twenty first century, and she was nineteen years old. Shouldn't she have overcome these jitters years ago? Then the rest of her emerged from the bedroom, and Travis forgot his irritation. He forgot everything but the woman standing in front of him now covered in a gauzy white nightie.

The spell from earlier returned, rendering him incapacitated and speechless, which wasn't a good thing if he wanted this night to progress to his liking. If one of them was going to make a move, it was going to have to be him, only it wasn't. He watched, mesmerized, as Caleigh stepped forward, rested her hands on his shoulders, and kissed him. She wasn't showing yet, so there was no baby mound to mar her perfect body. She was tall, almost as tall as him, with acres of creamy white skin, long dark hair, and brilliant green eyes. And she was his.

The kiss was innocent, yet full of emotion. Her purity and innocence disarmed him, making feel oddly vulnerable, as if the protective layers he had worked so hard to build were suddenly gone, leaving him as the soft-hearted idiot he had once been. There was a part of him that felt the panicked need to draw away, to erect the barrier between them again. But there was another, stronger part of him that was enchanted and entranced, drawn into whatever spell she was weaving. Caleigh was beauty and magic; she made him forget everything but her. So he stood still and allowed himself to be kissed again.

CHAPTER 4

"What should we name the baby?"

Caleigh's question drew Travis out of the Neverland between awake and asleep. His head was pillowed on her stomach, her hands were smoothing through his hair. "Dunno," he said, his voice heavy with grogginess. He had just been thinking that this was one of the top five nights of his life. There was no way he was going to impart that information to Caleigh, both because she would be upset it wasn't number one and because he didn't want her to know five was the sum total of the women he had been with, including her. He had an image to maintain. He was a marine—his bedpost should have more notches, or so he believed.

The night would have been number one except some of the other women had been more experienced and adventurous than Caleigh. Still, there had been something sweet between them. Maybe it was the time they were spending together now. This was definitely a first. There had never been much cuddling or conversation before. The realization struck that they would have many more nights together to ratchet up the adventure and experience and he smiled, feeling optimistic.

"If it's a boy, I've always liked the name Tucker."

He didn't say so, but he didn't really care. He hadn't given the issue much thought. Now that she brought it up, though…" If it's a girl, we can name her Margaret. Like my mom." His voice faded to a hoarse whisper and her hands stilled a few seconds before starting again. He wasn't sure what made him think of his mother. Maybe it was the wedding, or maybe it was the baby. She would have loved both, and Caleigh, too.

"How old were you when she died?"

"Nine."

Her right hand slipped to his bare back, caressing. He closed his eyes, enjoying the momentary easing of his ever-present pain. Would he ever get over the loss of his mother? No.

"What was she like?" Caleigh whispered.

"Fun, sweet, beautiful, kind, *attentive*." The usual dose of bitterness slipped into his tone on the last word.

"So your childhood was good before?" she prodded.

He should have been annoyed that she was stepping into what had always been a taboo subject, but for some reason tonight he was feeling mellow and didn't mind so much. "It was the best. Gage, Mom, and I, we had some great times."

"Were your parents divorced?"

"No, but when your father is career military, you learn to live life without him." His hand smoothed over her stomach, frowning. He didn't want that kind of life for his kid. How many times had he promised himself he would be there if he ever reproduced? Of course he hadn't pictured that happening for many more years.

"What was it like…after?" Caleigh asked.

He took a breath and held it. Did he really want to get into this with her? The old anger and resentment rose up, choking him. For a second he was tempted to tell her to mind her own business, but something held him back. Caleigh's curiosity was genuine, born from a desire to understand him. The least he could do was grant her access on their honeymoon.

"Dad couldn't be bothered to take time off and be with us, of course." Even though he could have taken family leave, he hadn't. He returned to work two days after the funeral and went on deployment a month later. "Gage and I were shipped to live with his sister, our aunt. She's okay. I don't know how she and the Admiral turned out so different. She wasn't Mom, but she did pretty well for someone who had two boys dumped in her lap. Of course I had Gage, and he took care of me a lot, so there wasn't much for her to do but provide room and board. But sometimes she went over and above, taking us to movies, concerts, museums, stuff like that, stuff our mom would have done."

"Did you live with her until you were out of school?"

"No, only until I was fourteen. Gage left home and the Admiral decided I needed his special brand of personal attention."

She must have sensed the tension in his voice because she tensed, too. "What does that mean?"

"I was not his ideal son in any way."

"Because you wanted to be a marine?" she guessed.

He expelled a humorless chuckle. "Babygirl, if that had been the issue, it would have been the least of our problems."

"What was it then?" she asked. He could tell she was smiling, probably from the endearment. It took so little to make Caleigh happy. What were people always yammering about? Marriage was easy, as far as he could tell.

"You have to understand Gage was always the heir apparent—tall, athletic, good in school, outgoing, popular. He had future navy officer written all over him." He sighed. "And then there was me."

"I'm not following," she said.

He tipped his head to look up at her. "What I'm about to tell you is a secret. Tell anyone and I'll never trust you again."

"I promise," she said, her verdant eyes rounded with solemnity.

She was so sincere he smiled before laying his head down and continuing. "I was fat."

"No way," she blurted.

"Yep. Hey." He glanced up in surprise as she pushed him onto his back and straddled his stomach.

"There is no way this body was ever fat," she said, running her fingertips over the ridges in his abdomen.

He was quickly losing his train of thought, but she seemed to be waiting for an answer. "I was, and I was cross-eyed. I had to have corrective surgery and wear a patch."

Her gaze met his, searching to see if he was telling the truth. "Aw," she said, sprawling on him and bestowing a kiss. It was a pity kiss. He tried to turn it into much more, but she pulled away. "And that's why your dad was mean to you, because you were a late bloomer?"

"But not only physically. I was shy, sensitive, too into comic books and video games. My only friend was Gage. Basically I was wrong in every way."

"So what did he do to you?" Her tone was filled with a protective ferocity he had never heard. She was angry at his dad. No one had ever been angry at the Admiral on his behalf before. Her unexpected support was heartening.

"First he put me on an exercise regimen," Travis said, not quite truthfully. First his father had crushed his spirit. After years of seeming indifference, Travis had been half hopeful he might finally get to know the father he only knew vicariously through Gage. But that wasn't to be. Instead their first real interaction had been blatant disapproval on the Admiral's part. He listed everything that was wrong with Travis—basically everything about him—and then told him how he intended to fix it. "And a diet. I went three years without sugar or soda. Instead I drank smoothies with whey powder."

"That's awful," Caleigh said.

He reached up and captured her hair, studying the silky tresses as he twined them through his fingers. He could have stopped there, but the same unknown power that had been guiding him all day compelled him to keep talking. "It was like he had a checklist. He threw away my game system, burned my comic books, and began inviting kids from my class to our house. By this time he was pretty high up in the navy, so our setup was pretty sweet—everything a teenage guy could want. A normal teenage guy, that is. There was basketball, a pool, billiards, foosball. I played along because no one wants to be a loser outcast, and suddenly I was popular." But popularity came with a price. Travis hadn't been an athlete, and he hadn't possessed whatever elusive quality makes some people popular by virtue of being alive. He had been forced to create his own niche, and he found it by unleashing his growing inner rage.

For years he had been the go-to guy for wild and crazy stunts. The trick was performing them undetected. It became a game, seeing how much illegal activity he could get away with right under the old man's nose. There was a part of him that had longed to get caught, if only to see his father's reaction. Would he be proud or chagrined? Would he realize he had sacrificed a good kid who toed the line but had no friends for one who routinely stole cars, smoked weed, and vandalized property all for the sake of popularity? It was an interesting question Travis pondered when he was feeling philosophical.

Going into the marines had seemed like the best way to get back at the Admiral, but maybe it had been a last-ditch effort at saving his own life.

"I'm so glad you turned out okay."

Okay? Was she joking? She thought he was okay? But her expression was sincere as always. For whatever reason, she believed in him. It would be interesting to know what she saw when she looked at him. Whatever it was, it wasn't something Travis had ever recognized when he looked in the mirror.

"I love you," Caleigh added.

There was no shyness or hesitation on her part, merely her normal earnest affection staring back at him. He wished he could say it back and mean it, but he couldn't. Maybe he was suffering an odd attack of conscience because all of a sudden he didn't want to say it if it wasn't real. He remained silent and kissed her, but Caleigh didn't complain.

CHAPTER 5

*K*elsey opened his mouth and Melly covered it with her fingers.

"I swear if you sing 'How Much is That Doggie in the Window' one more time, I am going home," she said.

With effort, he resisted the urge to kiss her fingers. "I'm simply trying to lighten the mood," Kelsey said.

"We're dog shopping. How much lighter could it get?"

"You tell me. You're the one who is turning this into a big thing. I don't understand what the big deal is. We go to the pet store, pick out a dog, and BAM! We're done," Kelsey said.

"First of all, I would never buy from a pet store. They get their dogs from puppy mills. Second, you cannot walk into a store and buy a dog. This is a big commitment, Kelsey. We need to make sure the dog has the right temperament, doesn't shed, fits well into both our homes."

His brow lowered at that last part. If he had his way, the dog would only have to fit into one home. Melly was the one being difficult, as always. "You're being difficult," he blurted, and quickly realized he was taking his life into his hands with that statement when she stopped short and rounded on him, hands on hips.

"If you want to get your own dog, then you can do it whatever haphazard way you want. You'll end up with a sick puppy that either dies in a month or eats your shoes for kicks but, hey, that's your choice. But any dog that is going to live in my home is going to be healthy, from a good family, and ready to live by my rules."

He opened his mouth, and she covered it again.

"If you say those sound like my rules for dating, then I'm leaving," she warned.

"What's the point of me being here if you know everything I'm going to say before I say it? Why don't you pick out the dog and show me when it's done?"

"Because I want your input," she said.

"Sure you do," he muttered.

"What was that?" she asked, rounding on him again.

He held up his hands in surrender and they continued walking. "I feel like we're hiking the Himalayas here," he said. They had been walking forever with no signs of civilization, trying to reach a dog breeder Melly read about online. She had apparently spent many hours researching responsible breeders in the area in her quest to find the perfect dog.

"You would know," Melly said.

Kelsey smiled. "That's one place I've never been, and I only climb mountains when I have to." They walked in comfortable silence a few more paces. "So you and Popeye seemed to hit it off the other night."

"What is it between marines and sailors?" Melly said. "I don't get the hostility. Aren't you guys part of the same branch?"

"They think they're so great," Kelsey said. "But we're the ones who do all the legwork while they stay on their fancy ships and planes."

"Gage was a SEAL. That probably included a lot of legwork," Melly pointed out.

"You can't know that for sure. He might not have seen much action."

She gave him a look. If he was a SEAL, then he saw action, and they both knew it. "Fine, whatever." He didn't want to hear any more glowing reviews, he simply wanted to find out what was going on. "So what's up? Did he ask you out? Did you say yes?"

Melly hesitated, which wasn't a good sign in Kelsey's opinion. "Kelsey, do you really want to do this? Can't we talk about something else?"

"You're the one who said we're still friends. We've always been up front about the people we're dating. Why should that change now?"

Melly sighed. "He asked me out. I said yes."

Kelsey's lips pressed together in a tight line, holding back a thundercloud of disapproval. There was no rational reason for him to disapprove beyond an inexhaustible supply of jealousy and sadness. "Oh."

She linked her arm through his. "Don't say that."

"What, oh? What's wrong with oh?"

"It's the way you said it, like I stabbed you through the heart. I'm not trying to hurt you."

You're doing an excellent job for someone who's not trying, he wanted to say, but he didn't. Melly was right, as usual. She wasn't trying to hurt him. She wanted to be with him as much as he wanted to be with her, only on her terms. And despite how much he wanted to be with her, he wasn't willing to bend, to give up his precious freedom and be tied down for the rest of his life.

"There," Melly said, excitement in her tone as she pointed at the horizon. A small farmhouse with a huge yard loomed ahead. The sound of yipping could be heard from where they stood.

"Exactly what kind of dog are we looking at here?" Kelsey asked.

"Labradoodles," Melly said.

"Labra what now?"

"Labradoodles, a cross between a Labrador and poodle. They have the temperament of a lab, the intelligence of a poodle, and they don't shed. This breeder has a sterling reputation for weaning and socialization as well as overall health."

"I understood exactly four words of that last sentence," Kelsey said.

Melly smiled and clasped his hand, tugging him forward. "C'mon."

They jogged the rest of the way down the rutted lane. Kelsey was glad they decided to park Melly's car at the end. She would no doubt have body damage if they had tried to drive down the long, pitted lane. Now that they were in sight of their target, Melly was transformed into a mass of quivering delight. If he had any idea her reaction to puppies was so strong, he would have bought her one years ago.

The farm's owner came outside to greet them as Melly spotted a pen of puppies languishing in the grass. "Oh," she exclaimed, letting go of his hand to dart over and make her inspection. Kelsey greeted the old woman as she hobbled down the steps. She began rattling off her puppies' statistics, but Melly wasn't listening. Apparently she had already made her selection.

"That one," she said, pointing. "I want that one."

Kelsey and the woman came over to look. He cocked his head, studying the puppy that looked nothing like the others.

"That's a Great Dane," the woman said. Her tone was that of someone imparting wisdom, as if Melly had made some mistake and she was clearing it up. "He's not one of mine. I took him on when he was about to be euthanized from the pound. I'm keeping him as a rescue; I couldn't in good conscience sell him when I don't know his history. And what I do know of it has been rough. He was removed from his mother too soon. He's bound to have problems."

"I want him," Melly said, staring at the huge black and white puppy that was walking all over the curly-haired dogs, mashing them into the ground with his massive paws.

"Don't Great Danes get sort of big?" Kelsey asked.

"Huge," the woman answered. "Easily a hundred pounds or more and four feet tall on all fours."

"And don't they shed?" Kelsey prodded.

"Horribly," the woman said.

"So what you're saying is this dog is going to be gigantic, a shedder, and most likely have social problems that will make him a shoe chewer or worse," Kelsey clarified.

"That's exactly what I'm saying. This dog is a question mark. I have no idea what his temperament, health, or size will be," the woman said.

Kelsey studied Melly's face as she studied the puppy. He sighed. "We'll take him," he said. He was rewarded when Melly threw her arms around him and jumped up and down in excitement, causing the Dane puppy to bay wildly.

A half an hour later—after signing a waiver that decreed they would in no way hold the breeder responsible for anything their new dog might do—they set off once again on the long hike to the car. The puppy was on a leash, but he didn't know that because he darted frantically from side to side, sniffing everything, jerking Melly's arm to and fro. He was already thirty pounds and came up to her shin. Melly was five feet and three inches. In a few months, the dog would be bigger than her.

Kelsey took the leash in his left hand and slipped his right arm around Melly. "What should we name this dog?"

"Rocky?" she suggested. One of the dog's lips was slightly hitched, reminiscent of Sylvester Stallone.

"I like it," he said.

Her arm eased around his waist and she looked up. "Thanks for not saying I told you so."

He gave her shoulders a squeeze. The truth was that he was feeling slightly jealous of the dog. Melly was willing to put aside her stringent rules for a cute puppy, but she wouldn't do the same for him. "Where is this bruiser going to stay tonight?"

"He should stay with you when you're in the states, that way you guys can bond," Melly said. Her tone was full of yearning, and he knew how much she was giving up by making the offer. She had fallen hard for the puppy and didn't want to be apart from him.

"I know nothing about puppies," Kelsey said.

"You'll learn," she assured him.

"Maybe you could teach me. I've heard they stay up all night the first few nights. You don't have work tomorrow, and I do. Could you stay and spell me with him until I get the hang of being a doggy daddy?"

"Okay," Melly said, her eyes alight with suppressed excitement. "I've never had a dog, and I've always wanted one. This is like a dream come true." They reached her car. She shoved her keys at him so she could hold the puppy on her lap which proved to be an acrobatic feat. The dog was all paws, and he was everywhere. Kelsey was glad there wasn't much traffic around town so he could enjoy the sight of her trying to wrangle the squirming beast.

They arrived at his house and let the dog inside, laughing when his feet gave out on the slippery vinyl flooring. He skittered, never breaking stride in his aim to sniff everything in sight, even though he couldn't find his footing.

"We should figure out a way to confine him or he's going to be everywhere and into everything," Melly said. They moved furniture around, creating a barrier to keep the dog in the living room. He whimpered, attempting to scamper over the furniture, but Kelsey set him down again with a firm "No." They stood back, watching the puppy as he got over his dejection and made peace with the arrangement.

"I thought Great Danes have pointy ears and short tales," Kelsey said.

"Not naturally. They're cut that way," Melly said.

Kelsey's mouth fell. "That's horrible. They cut their ears and tails off?"

"Well, some say it's not only aesthetically pleasing, but serves a purpose. Their ears are long and don't allow for air circulation, harboring moisture that can cause infection. And their tails are powerful, like dinosaur tails."

"I don't want that done to him," Kelsey declared.

"I don't either, but it's too late anyway. He's too old." The breeder assured them the dog had already eaten and wouldn't need to eat again until the next day, so Melly retrieved water and set it on the floor for him. He lapped at it a few times before quickly knocking it over with one of his too-big paws.

"He reminds me of me when I was a teenager," Kelsey said. "All hands and feet and no idea how to use them."

"I can't imagine you clumsy," Melly said. He had the grace of a natural athlete but she didn't allow herself to dwell too long on his physique. Her new awareness of him in that way was too potent and too difficult to keep suppressed. Instead she turned her attention to cleaning up the spilled water. "It's clean in here," she noticed, surveying the usually messy room with a glance.

"Truck is finally taking over. With Nick and Travis gone, he has an easier time of cleaning. He's sort of obsessive about it." They sank into the couch.

"Are you guys managing the rent okay with only the two of you?"

Kelsey shrugged. "For now, but it's about to be a moot point. Truck's going to pop the question." He frowned, scanning the large space. "I should probably start looking for somewhere else to live." There weren't many options for a single man who lived so much of his life overseas, mostly depressing bachelor apartments or base housing. Both were small, cold, and empty. This house, though not grand by any standards, had actually felt like home. "Truck asked me to help him think of a way to propose, but it's turning out to be harder than I thought. Do you have any ideas?"

Melly shook her head. "It's one thing to ask from input from your buddies, and another to have a woman give her advice. I don't think Shelby would like it if I ordered her proposal. You guys are on your own."

She was probably right. Women had weird rules about stuff like that. "What about you? What's your perfect proposal?" He thought she would like something simple, but Melly was full of surprises. She might be one of those women who needed a scavenger hunt ending on national television or something.

"Sincere," she said. "I don't care what it is, as long as he means it." The puppy put his paws on her knees and she picked him up, allowing him to cuddle in her lap. He harrumphed as he settled into a more comfortable position and quickly fell asleep.

"Great, he snores," Kelsey said. He whispered, not wanting to wake the puppy for fear of another dose of out-of-control energy.

"He's adorable," Melly declared. "I love everything about him." She gazed at the dog with such a look of pure devotion that Kelsey was once again jealous.

"I know the feeling," he said. He was probably looking at her the same way she was looking at the dog. She glanced up with a smile that faltered as she took in his meaning. He wanted to set the dog aside, take her in his arms, and kiss her until she gave up whatever notion was keeping them apart. But he didn't. Instead he put his arm around her and turned on the television, settling in for a long night of puppy fatherhood.

CHAPTER 6

For two weeks, Caleigh and Travis's marriage was like something from a storybook. For the first three days, they were on their honeymoon. Travis somehow managed to go without getting drunk for the duration, a record for him. They returned home and began arranging their new rental house.

It was tiny, but had a lot of charm—or at least Caleigh told him it did. To him, it looked exactly like every other house, only smaller. But she was pleased with it, and her enthusiasm was catching. He actually found himself feeling excited as they unloaded their things and began unpacking. Their furniture consisted of a ragtag assortment of hand-me-downs from Caleigh's parents and Gage. Travis expected Caleigh to demand some new stuff, but she didn't mention a word about it except to say at some point they would need to get baby furniture.

Travis couldn't understand his new happiness. It was unlike him to feel content and so of course it couldn't last. After two weeks of almost blissful happiness, he came home and found Caleigh in what was going to be the nursery. She was painting the wall with some type of mural. He stood back to admire her work before she realized he was there. She was a talented artist, something he hadn't known until after they were married. And she was musical, too. She played piano—

an old one someone in her church donated—and guitar. In the evenings when he sat and watched sports, Caleigh pulled out her guitar and sat beside him on the couch, lightly picking out a gentle melody he didn't recognize.

Her guitar playing was another of those thing that landed somewhere between enjoyment and annoyance for him. On the one hand, the music was pretty and it was sort of cool that she played. On the other, couldn't she sit quietly and let him enjoy ESPN in peace?

"Hey," he said, startling her so she jumped. Her hand flew to her hair before remembering she was holding a brush. She set it aside and stood, darting close to kiss him. She kissed him every day when he came home, greeting him with the same enthusiasm and reverence one might give a long-awaited celebrity.

"Hey," she said after the kiss was over. "I missed you."

She was always saying stuff like that, always telling him she loved him, missed him, enjoyed being with him. And she never seemed to notice or mind when he didn't say it in return.

"What's for supper?" he asked.

"BBQ bacon cheeseburgers," she said.

His mouth began to water. Another pleasant surprise about Caleigh was that she was an amazing cook. He had tasted Ashleigh's cooking, and their mother's food, and he believed Caleigh was better than both of them. This he had no trouble telling her, but she didn't believe him. She would laugh and bat him away, usually saying something like, "You're saying that because you have to." Proof she didn't know him at all; Travis never said anything because he had to.

She had also made potato salad and apple pie. He pinched a bite of the salad while she began frying the burgers. "You should open a restaurant," he said.

She glanced up with a vague smile, and he tamped down his annoyance. Any time he mentioned her getting a job she gave him that same look, as if he were an idiot and she had no intention of seeking work. At some point they were going to have to address the issue of their finances, but for the first time in forever Travis was loathe to upset the peace. He simply wanted to enjoy this newfound sense of fulfillment and hope it might be permanent. Maybe this was why people got married, because marriage was actually sort of nice. His laundry was clean and in his drawers every day. Delicious food was on the table every night. A beautiful woman lay within his grasp, ripe for the taking. Yes, marriage was turning out to be much better than he expected.

He pulled out a beer and they sat down to eat. So far he hadn't felt the overwhelming urge to have a night on the town and get wasted. His nightly beer at supper seemed to be enough, and he chuckled at the family man he had turned into. Caleigh didn't drink, of course, but neither did she disapprove of him doing so.

Supper was delicious, and he told her so. Her cheeks warmed with delight and he got caught up staring at her, realizing anew how very pretty she was. What she was doing with him was a baffling mystery.

"I was thinking maybe we could go shopping for baby furniture this weekend," she suggested. "I heard of this thrift store that sells really good things. Even if they don't have what we want, we could leave our names and they could call when something comes in."

"I thought I told you I'm going away this weekend," he said.

She froze. "You're on assignment?"

He shook his head. He was sure he had mentioned this weekend to her. Hadn't she been listening? "I'm going away with my buddies. Sort of a belated bachelor party."

Her blinks became more rapid while the rest of her remained frozen. "You're going to Vegas?" she whispered.

"Yeah, Caleigh, I'm sure I told you about this."

"That was before we got married," she said.

"And..." he prompted.

"We're married now," she said.

He sighed. He had no idea what she was trying to say. Why couldn't women come out and say what they meant? He hadn't taken her for one to play games. "What is the big deal? Can you tell me so I can stop trying to guess?"

"Married men don't go to Vegas for drunken orgies with their friends," Caleigh said.

He was shocked, both by the vehement anger in her tone and by her use of the word "orgies." He didn't know she knew what that word meant. "Orgies? There won't be any orgies." He thought that was the end of the discussion, and he returned to his burger.

"But there will be women, right?" Caleigh pressed. "Like those stripper shows. Don't try to pretend that's not what you're going for."

"So? What's the big deal?"

"The big deal is that married men don't go to those kinds of shows. That's cheating."

He laughed, a frustrated puff of exasperation. "Caleigh, do you think all the men in the audience are single? No. And it's not cheating if there's no touching."

"You think this is funny?" she said. She was practically yelling now. Travis stared at her in amazement. He had never seen her angry before. "This is not funny, and it is cheating. How would you feel if I went to a show full of nude men?"

The thought of Caleigh at such a show was so ridiculous he couldn't give it credence. "You're blowing this out of proportion. It's not that big a deal."

"It's a big deal to me. I don't want you to go."

Up until now, he had been merely amused by her jealous display, but now she was treading on dangerous ground. "You can't tell me what to do."

"I'm not telling, I'm asking. Please don't go."

"And say what? That my wife doesn't want me to go?"

"Yes," she said.

"I'm not whipped."

"So the opinion of your friends means more to you than my opinion?"

"No, but you don't get to tell me what to do. You don't get a say in the way I live my life."

Her jaw went slack with a wounded expression that annoyed him. Anger was easier to deal with than hurt feelings. "Then what is this marriage all about?" she asked. "Two separate people living two separate lives? Because that's not what I thought we were doing here. I thought we were making something together. I thought we were becoming a family."

"The baby isn't even born yet," Travis said.

"We don't need the baby to be a family."

He frowned, confused. She was speaking in riddles again. "Caleigh, men go to Vegas all the time. If they didn't, it wouldn't exist. Don't make this into more than it is, it's a getaway with my friends."

"A getaway with your friends is a weekend hiking the Appalachian Trail. This is cheating. Don't try to water it down with semantics." She pushed away from the table and went to their room, closing the door quietly behind her.

Travis stared at the closed door, stunned. What had that been about? Since when did Caleigh get angry about stuff? And since when did she have a backbone? He should have known her Puritan upbringing would rear its ugly head sooner or later. Clearly she didn't understand how it was. She must be picturing him hiring a hooker or something. They would be in a group, watching a show. She would come around eventually or she would get over it.

He shrugged, turning his attention back to his meal.

* * *

CALEIGH DIDN'T GET over it, though, at least not completely. After a couple days of sullen silence, she eventually began talking to him again, but the sad puppy expression didn't leave her face. Travis was as annoyed by her as he was to his reaction to her. There was a pinprick of conscience that wouldn't leave him alone. She was infecting him with her holier-than-thou opinions, and he didn't like it at all. True, neither of the friends who were going to Vegas with him was married, but he knew married guys who went all the time. And some of them didn't stop at going to shows, some of them hired personal entertainment. When he thought of himself in comparison to them, he was practically an angel. Why couldn't Caleigh see it that way?

She didn't kiss him goodbye, but then he hadn't really expected her to. She did say goodbye, which was something, he supposed. And then an unwelcome surprise awaited him at the airport.

"Wait up," an agonizingly familiar voice said. Travis turned to see Kelsey jogging behind him.

"What are you doing here?" Travis asked.

"I'm coming with. The other guys didn't tell you?"

"No. Why are you coming?" Travis asked, his tone full of suspicion. Had Nick ordered him to make sure Travis didn't get out of hand? Or, worse, had Caleigh asked him to come along? It was no secret she and Kelsey had a sort of big brother/little sister bond going on.

"Are you kidding? Guys weekend in Vegas? It's like a dream come true." Kelsey looked and sounded perfectly innocent, but it was hard to tell because he was a good actor.

"You don't drink anymore," Travis pointed out.

"Is drinking really going to be the highlight of this weekend?" Kelsey asked, grinning.

Travis's accepting nod was half-hearted in response. Maybe Kelsey actually did want to go for the fun of it. They had been on their way to developing a real bond before Kelsey gave up drinking and Travis started dating Caleigh.

The other two guys showed up and, to Travis's chagrin, looked at Kelsey like he was some sort of demigod. Snipers inspired a certain amount of awe among younger marines. Travis had gotten over his awe after working so closely with them and realizing they were normal guys. Truth be told, he enjoyed his own amount of notoriety for being point man on their team. It was a coveted position, and his father's name and influence had no doubt had something to do with why Travis was given the assignment, as much as he hated to admit it. He had never purposely used Caldwell's connections to further his own career, but to his dismay the connections seemed to happen without his consent.

"Murphy, Stokes," Kelsey said. Travis had to fight down his gag reflex at Murphy and Stokes' over-the-top responses to the fact that Kelsey actually knew their names.

"So, you were actually in that dogfight that killed Lolly a few months ago," Murphy said. "That had to be crazy, huh?"

Now Travis's irritation turned to amusement. There were two ways to get on Kelsey's bad side: one was to mention Lolly, and the other was to mention his sister, Melly.

"Crazy," Kelsey said. "But my therapist tells me I'm on the road to recovery." He turned and stowed his bag in the overhead compartment while Murphy and Stokes gave each other a look, trying to figure out of Kelsey was serious. Travis knew he was, but he wasn't about to volunteer that information. Not only did he not want to have a gossip session about another man, but it felt disloyal to dish on one of his teammates.

By the time the plane took off, Travis was already regretting the trip. Perhaps it was immature, but Murphy and Stokes were supposed to be his friends, the friends he made to get away from his team. And yet they were panting after his teammate's attention like the geeky kids in high school had followed after Gage. And, like Gage, Kelsey was giving them their due, favoring them with stories of his more hair-raising exploits. To Travis's further annoyance, all of them took place before he became the team's point man.

By the time the plane touched down in Vegas, Travis was ready to turn around and go back home again. He pulled out his phone and stared at it, debating whether or not to call Caleigh.

"C'mon, man, you're not wussing out on us now, are you? We just got here," Stokes said.

Travis turned to find all three of them watching him. Kelsey's eyebrow was raised in a challenging expression that was somehow different than Murphy and Stokes, as if he would be impressed if Travis made the call and went back home. That, more than anything, caused him to stuff the phone back in his pocket. "Are you kidding? The night is young," he said.

CHAPTER 7

Melly groaned when her phone rang at six in the morning. It was summer vacation, but Kelsey had never cared about that. Vacations, weekends, days when she had the flu, middle of the night, middle of the day—time was meaningless when he decided he wanted to talk.

"Hello," she said, trying to induce some guilt by letting him hear how groggy she was.

"I'm old," he started.

"What clued you in?" she asked.

"Six hours at two strip clubs," he replied.

"I *really* do not want to hear what those women did to wear you out," Melly said. She started to hang up, but he preempted her.

"Not like that. I meant the opposite. There was a time when I was a new recruit that an evening spent watching scantily-clad women shimmy on a pole would have been the height of cultural awareness for me. Tonight all I could think was that there's probably a high rate of cancer with so much silicone in their systems. The smoke made me cough. The booze made me gag, and the women made me sad. They looked so…objectified. What's wrong with me?"

"You've grown," Melly said, her voice warming with approval.

He sighed. "Life was simpler when I had no moral compass. What have you done to me with your wholesomeness and good character? I'm forever tainted by your high standards."

"For what it's worth, I like you better this way," Melly said. "How's our boy?"

"Stupid, but sleeping it off alone. I don't know how I pulled the short straw on this one. Want to know the least fun job in the world? Babysitting a marine who's bent on self-destruction."

"You're fighting the good fight," Melly said. "Don't lose faith. Think of Caleigh."

"I have been, and so has he. If there was anyone having less fun than me tonight, it was him. He doesn't know it, or he won't admit it. What's wrong with this kid? Why can't he see what he has in her? What they could have together? I'm not a promoter of young marriage, but since it's already a done deal, he might as well make the best of it. Who goes to Vegas two weeks after his wedding? Even I was never that dumb." She took a breath and he talked over her. "No rebuttal from the peanut gallery, please. How's our dog?"

"He misses you. He keeps looking expectantly toward the door, and he won't stay in his bed. He's been sleeping with me."

"Lucky mutt," he said as another irrational wave of jealousy overtook him. He resented the dog almost as much as he loved him. Melly's instinct about the pup had been correct. Despite being too big and too spirited, Rocky was a great dog with a big heart. He made Kelsey laugh and kept him from feeling anxious when ill thoughts tried to intrude. His therapist, Marilyn, heartily approved of the new pet, especially after he took Rocky to a session and introduced him.

"Kelsey," Melly said.

"Hmm," Kelsey replied. His blinks were becoming heavier. Staying up all night to party wasn't as easy as it once was. He was exhausted.

"You wouldn't go to a strip club if you were married, would you?"

"Of course not," he said, half offended she would even ask.

"And you're single, fully allowed to go to one if you want. But you didn't enjoy it. Right?"

"Right," he said. He felt she was leading somewhere, but he couldn't see where. "What's your point?"

"Maybe that you're fighting desperately to hang on to your single status so you won't have to give up your coveted freedom. But it doesn't seem like you're enjoying freedom very much. I should go, the dog is whining. I love you." She hung up, just like that.

Now Kelsey was once again wide awake, staring at the ceiling. Tricky Melly, planting thoughts in his head he would have to turn over and examine until he figured them out. What was the point of staying single if he wasn't having fun? He rolled over and punched his pillow, irritated with Melly, himself, Travis, and the world in general. He was not ready to get married, and that was that. True, the last few months without Melly had been a misery, but maybe he wasn't trying hard enough to have fun. From now on, fun was his number one goal. He was drifting off when he came to the realization fun had been his number one goal his whole life and it still hadn't made him happy.

* * *

Back home in North Carolina, Caleigh was equally miserable. What was wrong with her marriage that her husband of two weeks felt he had to go away and ogle other women? He would no doubt come back and be disappointed with her. She had never been anyone's idea of busty. Maybe that was the problem. Maybe he didn't like her body. Or maybe it was her lack of experience. He wouldn't say how many women he had been with before her, but the number was probably massive. Caleigh must be a disappointment in every way. How else to explain his abandonment?

She was baffled. To her, things had been going well, like she always imagined. Travis went to work while she kept house. He came home and they spent their evenings together. The past two weeks had been like something from a dream. Caleigh cherished her time with him even more because she knew it was inevitable he would be going on assignment soon. Their time together was precious, but apparently she was the only one who felt that way. Apparently Travis preferred the company of his friends and naked women he didn't know.

A few self-pitying tears slipped out and she wiped them away. At least Kelsey was there making sure he didn't get into trouble, a fact that both heartened and annoyed her. For all of her life, people had been taking care of Caleigh, hovering over her, protecting her, making sure she didn't get hurt. She knew it came from a place of love, but at the same time it was maddening. What was wrong with her that people thought she couldn't stand on her own? Why did everyone else in the world get to stand on their own two feet while Caleigh constantly had people swooping in to save her? She knew she should be grateful for their care. Lots of people lived their whole lives without knowing the kind of love she had known from birth. But sometimes that same love was stifling.

Like now with Kelsey. She hadn't asked him to go and keep an eye on Travis. In fact, she had asked him not to go, not wanting Travis to think Kelsey was her spy. But Kelsey said it was Nick's decision and out of her hands, a team thing because they didn't want Travis to get into any kind of trouble that would affect his career. Caleigh knew that wasn't true, though. Nick may have ordered Kelsey to go, but it wasn't for the team; it was for her. She was almost twenty, married, pregnant, and still her family kept diving to her rescue. Maybe it was because they knew something she didn't—maybe she was incapable of making it on her own.

She curled into a ball and wept, sure life couldn't possibly hurt any more than it did now. Unknown to her, she would soon be proved wrong.

THE PLANE RIDE home was quiet. Murphy and Stokes each had a hangover. Stokes clutched his airsick bag like a lifeline. Kelsey wasn't hungover, but he was quiet for whatever reason. Travis thought he was acting odd, even for him.

He had been suspicious of Kelsey's arrival, knowing he was sent to keep an eye on him. His suspicions grew when he sat back the first night and surveyed the scene with blatant distaste and disapproval. But then the second night he transformed into their leader, taking them to secret clubs he had visited years before when he came on some notorious bender with Ashton and Nick. Travis was baffled by the transformation, and even more baffled by Kelsey's mood because he was oddly angry. It was as if he had something he was trying to prove, but the longer the night went on, the angrier he became.

There was something to be said for the way he cycled through women, though. Travis had always had to work for whatever girl he wanted. Not so Kelsey. He was the center of the room wherever they went. All it took was some eye contact and a nod and the women came running. Murphy and Stokes no doubt thought Kelsey was as legendary as they had always heard, but Travis knew better because after a few minutes of flirting and conversation, Kelsey sent the women away, disgusted again. Except the last one.

She had been a dead ringer for Melly, only taller and less curvaceous. But she had the same dark skin and long dark hair. This one was almost prettier, in Travis's opinion. Melly was a little too curvy for his tastes; he liked his women taller and slimmer, more like Caleigh. Kelsey had talked to her for two solid hours, flirting and laughing. Travis kept waiting for him to take the girl back to his room, his disgust and irritation growing as time went on. He didn't get it. Kelsey was single. The woman was gorgeous and obviously interested. Where was the problem?

He decided to find out when the woman went to the bathroom, only he did it in his usual abrasive style, temporarily forgetting how touchy Kelsey was on the subject of Melly.

"What's the matter? Are you afraid this one won't let you seal the deal, either?" he had asked and then ducked because Kelsey took a swing at him. The swing took Travis by surprise, but not as much as the realization of how much he wanted to fight back. He was sick of Kelsey's back and forth friendship, sick of the way his teammates looked down on him, sick of the way everyone compared him to Lolly, to Gage, sick of not measuring up, of feeling angry. He was sick of everything. He swung back, Kelsey ducked, and that's when Murphy and Stokes intervened. Even though they were both almost too drunk to stand, the ability to break up a fight must be written into Marine DNA. They pulled the two teammates apart with commands to hash it out later after they sobered up, but Kelsey and Travis looked at each other, knowing the truth: neither of them was drunk.

Travis had left then, going back to his room in disgust. The downside to that arrangement was that he wasn't there when the Melly doppelganger returned. Had Kelsey taken her back to his hotel? He was curious, but not enough to ask Kelsey and risk another almost-fight. At this point he simply wanted to get home and…And what? *See Caleigh.* He might as well admit it—he missed his wife. How had that happened? Somehow her gentle sweetness had crept under his skin, settling somewhere near but not quite in his heart.

CHAPTER 8

*C*aleigh was waiting for Travis when he stepped through security. She looked a little uncertain, and a whole lot sad, and Travis felt another unfamiliar stab of conscience. He had hurt her, but he hadn't really meant to. Why did she have to be such a prude?

In apology for whatever hurt he had caused her, he kissed her long and deep, not caring who saw. Stokes, Murphy, and Kelsey paused behind him, waiting to get by while he blocked the path and created a bottleneck of repressed traffic.

Caleigh responded, but not with her usual wholehearted enthusiasm. He began to think it might be fun to spend the evening coaxing a better response when she spoke, poking a hole in his idea.

"Gage is coming for supper."

"Tonight?" Travis said.

"He was coming to spend the evening with Melly, but she's sick."

Travis moved aside as Kelsey jostled forward. "Melly's sick? What's wrong with her?"

"Stomach virus or something. I don't know," Caleigh said. "We should get home so I can finish cooking." She turned and walked away, not waiting for Travis to keep pace. He trotted to catch up, darting glances at her profile as they walked. He hadn't taken her for the sulky type, but obviously he was wrong because she was definitely pouting.

"What did you do all weekend?" he asked.

"Shopped, painted, cleaned, hung out. Stuff."

"Sounds busy," he said.

"It was a blast," she said with no inflection. She jerked open the door and stormed through, leaving him frowning at her backside.

"I didn't take you for a pouter," he said, catching up with her once again.

"You didn't corner the market on bad attitudes," she said. She lobbed the car keys at his chest and he easily caught them, staring at her in surprise. This new Caleigh was kind of a pain, but she was also slightly more enjoyable than the one with the unkillable smile and peppy good cheer. This one he could relate to, at least.

They drove home in silence, but for Travis it was a thoughtful silence. He was glad to know his wife wasn't perfect. She had a temper and she could hold a grudge. Good. He was growing weary of the cheerleader/nun version of her that he had dated and married. A woman in a temper was much easier for him to relate to than a woman who was constantly happy.

Gage was waiting in their driveway when they arrived home. Caleigh found her smile as she gave his brother a hug. Travis narrowed his eyes, ready to call her on faking a good mood, but he realized she wasn't faking—she was genuinely glad to see Gage. That was true to form in his experience; women loved his brother. And why shouldn't they? Gage always knew the right thing to say and do to make a woman smile, while Travis always knew the right thing to say and do to make a woman angry.

Caleigh hooked her arm through Gage's and led him inside, giving him a tour of their tiny rental. She paused in front of the baby's room. "I'm not finished yet, but I'm far enough along that you'll be able to tell what the end product will look like." She opened the door with a flourish. Gage stepped inside and whistled.

"You did all this yourself, Caleigh?" he asked.

Travis stood on his toes to see over their heads. He wasn't sure what the big deal was. There were some murals on the wall, and they were pretty good, but the Louvre wouldn't be calling anytime soon.

"I did," Caleigh said, sounding pleased by his complimentary tone. "I mixed the paint myself because I couldn't find the colors I wanted, and then I did a special wash on this wall to mute the colors. Some of them have gloss so they stand out a little more." She ran her finger over a dusky-colored apple on one wall.

"My niece or nephew is one lucky baby to get to live in this room," Gage said.

"You know we can't take this room with us when we move," Travis interjected. He didn't see the point of putting so much work into a rental.

Caleigh froze him with a look. "That doesn't mean we have to live with boring white walls while we're here."

He held up his hands in surrender because she looked ready to leap at him and wring his neck. "Just saying," he said.

Gage cleared his throat in the awkward silence. "Is that beef I smell? Please tell me my nose isn't wrong, and we're actually having some form of red meat tonight."

Caleigh found her smile once more. "I made a roast with twice-baked potatoes, a vegetable casserole, and peach cobbler with ice cream for dessert."

Gage patted his stomach and glanced at his brother. "You're going to have to start doubling up on your training if you want to keep fitting in that uniform."

Weight was a sensitive issue for Travis, having spent so many of his formative years as the roly-poly fat kid. He pressed his hand to his stomach to make sure there was no encroaching fat. "I eat healthy at work." When Caleigh frowned, he realized he had made it sound like he begrudged her delicious food, which wasn't true. But he did have to eat lighter when he wasn't home in order to avoid packing on pounds of unwanted fat. He spent his days training, but it wasn't the same as being in the field. There he would never worry about extra calories, and he would kill for some of her cooking. He had never been good at undoing his blunders, though, so he simply turned and walked from the room.

Gage and Caleigh followed. Gage was chattering now in that way he had of trying to cover for Travis. Usually Travis didn't mind, but when it was directed at his wife, he felt oddly proprietary. It wasn't Gage's job to make amends for him with Caleigh. It was his job, even though he had no idea how to do it.

Caleigh finished the tour of their tiny abode. Gage oohed and ahhed at all the appropriate times, complimenting Caleigh on how well she had done with so little to work with. Travis surveyed the space through his brother's eyes and was surprised by what he saw. The place did look nice. Despite the small size and shabby furniture, it looked cozy and homey. It was perpetually clean and always smelled good. Travis hadn't lived somewhere that smelled good since he left his aunt's house. Making things smell nice must be a female talent.

He sat at the table while Caleigh fussed in the kitchen. Gage stood to help her, making Travis feel like even more of a heel. He had come to expect her to wait on him. Why, though? He didn't think of himself as one of those old-fashioned men who believed the woman should do all the housework. But Caleigh had done it, willingly and effortlessly. And he had let her, firmly believing that she enjoyed serving him because that was the type of person she was. But what if she didn't? What if she wanted him to help set the table and he sat like a lazy loser, doing nothing night after night?

He had grown used to being compared to Gage. In their father's eyes, and in the eyes of the world, Travis would never measure up. He had long ago stopped caring about the comparison. But this was different. Seeing himself compared to Gage through Caleigh's lens was painful. He realized she had gotten the short shaft when she married him, but he didn't want her to realize it, especially not in comparison to perfect Gage who was doing and saying all the right things while Travis bungled everything like usual. Why couldn't he be the type of person who complimented without making it sound like an insult? Why couldn't he be the type of person who always knew the right thing to do and did it? Why instead was he the type of person who seemed bent on making those around him miserable? It was all well and good to defy authority and make his father miserable, but Caleigh hadn't done anything to him. Why did he have to bring her down?

Of course feeling miserable made him want to make others miserable, so he spent the meal in surly silence as Gage and Caleigh exchanged pleasant and perfect conversation. An uncomfortable realization was growing in his midsection, one that told him his brother and his wife were a much better match. Travis should have married a reformed hooker or someone like one of the strippers he had spent the weekend watching. Someone who didn't expect too much, someone who knew and understood they were getting a faulty model in him. Instead he received a paragon of beauty and perfection. He had inadvertently married the female version of his brother, and wasn't that a kick in the teeth?

He stood at the door with Caleigh as they said goodbye to Gage. From the outside looking in, they looked like any happy couple saying goodbye to family. But as soon as Gage was gone, the ensuing silence was heavy. Caleigh turned to clean the kitchen and Travis followed.

"What are you doing?" she asked, eyeing him with suspicion.

"Helping," he said.

Her lashes fluttered in surprise. "Why?"

"Because it's not 1954," he said, which made her laugh. He smiled and a little of the tension eased between them.

They worked in silence that was somewhere between comfortable and oppressive. "I'm going to bed," Caleigh announced when they were finished. "I'm exhausted."

Travis's ears perked up at the mention of the word "bed." Did she mean that how he hoped she meant it, or was she really going to sleep? Sleep, he decided when she pulled out her rattiest nightshirt. This was the first night since their marriage she hadn't worn a filmy piece of lingerie. He would be lying if he said he didn't miss the frilly concoctions. He had grown used to seeing her beautiful body on display every night. The faded, stretched shirt that hung to her knees wasn't quite the same, but Caleigh was still beautiful and he had missed her. He took a step forward and kissed her.

She froze, going rigid in his arms. "I'm really tired," she said.

He wasn't a marine for nothing. Defeat didn't come easily, and so he kissed her again, massaging the base of her spine until she started to relax.

"I think I want to go to sleep," she said, but her tone sounded more forced, less convinced.

"Mm, hmm," he muttered, kissing her again as he backed her to the bed.

* * *

SOMETIME LATER CALEIGH lay staring up at the ceiling. Beside her Travis was snoring softly, but why shouldn't he be? He got what he wanted. There was no need for him to stay awake. The fact that he had so easily bent her to his will without so much as an apology didn't escape Caleigh's notice. She was disgusted with herself. Why was she so weak and stupid when it came to him?

She was determined that when he came home, she wouldn't cave. They would have a serious talk about the issues between them. But then he stepped off the plane looking like the poster child for Marine recruits, and he kissed her, really kissed her, as if he had missed her as much as she missed him—doubtful since he had been well occupied with other women. She was as incensed about that as she was the fact that she gave in so easily. She had a legitimate reason to be angry, to say no when he approached her, and yet she couldn't. It was maddening.

The oddest part of her new arrangement was that she had never factored physical intimacy into marriage. She knew it was a part of marriage, of course, but her family had never emphasized that side of things. For the Desmonds, it was all about friendship, loyalty, dedication, hard work—all of the things that made relationships run smoothly and last. Her mother was fond of saying physical intimacy in marriage was God's gift, but that was as much as she ever said on the subject. Until the last couple of years, Caleigh had no idea what it even entailed until Ashleigh sat her down and explained the birds and the bees. At that, her sister had stammered, blushed, and used a lot of euphemisms. So it came as something of a shock to Caleigh that physical intimacy should now be the most successful part of her new marriage. She couldn't talk to her husband, couldn't relate to him in any emotional sort of way, but they definitely had chemistry.

Her tears came unbidden, but still Travis didn't stir. Why would he? He probably couldn't care less if she cried her eyes out, so long as she was still a willing participant when the lights went out. Caleigh felt like she was growing up before her own eyes, and she didn't like it. Even when she had found out she was pregnant, she hadn't lost the glittery enthusiasm of clueless youth. She'd had happy dreams of the way it would be with Travis. Now reality was setting in. She would raise the baby alone, like she was in a marriage alone. Travis didn't love her. Sometimes she doubted whether or not he even liked her.

The more pertinent question in Caleigh's mind was whether or not she loved him. She was attracted to him for sure. He was nice looking without being the handsomest guy she'd ever known, but there was something about his cocky swagger that reeled her in. For better or worse, Travis was who he was with no apologies. For Caleigh, who was a people pleaser and always had been, there was something galvanizing about his take-no-prisoners attitude. Like him or not he didn't care, and no one's opinion was going to change him. She gave a rueful little smile at the irony of being included in that statement. Caleigh's opinion wouldn't change him, either. If she didn't approve of his life choices, he didn't care, and he certainly wasn't willing to change. He had proved that this weekend.

She shuddered and sniffled. Travis reached for her and she froze. Was he awake? As much as she wanted comfort, having him see her this way felt like losing a battle somehow. "Babygirl," he muttered, but his eyes were closed. His face nuzzled her neck as he planted a kiss on her collarbone before becoming dead weight and crushing her arm. He began to snore again. Caleigh pressed her face to his shoulder, letting her tears soak his shirt. If the only comfort he had to offer happened while he was unconscious, then she would still take it because she needed it that desperately.

* * *

MEANWHILE KELSEY WAS TRYING to talk himself out of offering comfort to Melly. Even as he drove to her house, he told himself he wouldn't. He was still in denial about what he was doing until she opened the door.

"What's wrong with you?" he asked.

"How is it we're a military unit and yet no one can keep a secret?" Melly asked.

"Why would it be a secret you're sick?" He bypassed her when she made no motion to move aside.

She closed the door and followed him into her living room while Rocky darted boisterously around their ankles. "It's not a secret, per se. I didn't want anyone making a big deal out of it. How was the rest of your weekend?" She lay on the couch, petting Rocky's nose when he nuzzled her shoulder.

Miserable. "Great. Fun. Awesome." He smiled to make his words more convincing, but Melly's eyes were closed, so she missed it.

"Mm," she murmured. "Sounds better than mine. I hate being sick on vacation. It's like a double punishment." She looked and sounded so weak Kelsey's irrational anger fled. He knelt in front of her and pressed his hand to her clammy forehead.

"Can I get you anything?"

For a second, her usual Melly barriers were down, and she looked at him with so much longing his mouth went dry.

"Melly," he croaked.

The barriers went back up and she smiled. "No, I'm fine, but I haven't fed Rocky yet. And if you're feeling really generous, you could take him out."

"I could take him home with me," Kelsey suggested. Like a child of divorce, the dog split time between their homes, never knowing where he was going to be sleeping because Kelsey never knew when he was going to be called away. Life had been quiet recently which was never a good sign. It usually meant something big was coming.

"I suppose," Melly said, winding her fingers in Rocky's fur. "I miss him when he's gone. Sometimes I wonder how we ever got by without him."

It was on the tip of Kelsey's tongue to say something witty, but she was right; how had they survived so long without a dog as lovably sweet as Rocky? "I don't like leaving you alone when you're sick."

She transferred her hand from the dog to him. "It's a stomach bug; I'm fine. Plus Shelby will be home soon. Any luck finding proposal inspiration?"

"I'm working on it," Kelsey said, not wanting to give away any secrets before the big event.

She smiled. "It's nice Truck wants to do it up big. She'll like that."

"I hope. She's sort of grown on me. She's very normal for all she's been through."

"She doesn't want to be a victim, she wants to be normal. She works so hard to not be afraid, but I think being married to Truck will be good for her, give her a little more security."

"Except for those times when we're out of the country," Kelsey pointed out.

"Yes, but it's not only physical security. There's the security of knowing you belong to someone."

It was impossible to miss the hint of longing in her tone. "You belong to me, Melly. We're family."

"I appreciate the sentiment, but it's not really the same, is it? If something happens to you, I don't have the security of your pension to see me through. Shelby will have that after she's married. And then there's the support group. There's no group for friends of soldiers. You have to marry one to join that club. And there are a thousand other unspoken things that signify belonging to someone."

Kelsey felt the noose tightening. "Why are you doing this? Why are you guilting me?"

"I'm not," Melly said, peeved. "I'm explaining to you why I want marriage. It's not the same saying someone is your family. The proof is in the pudding, as your grandmother would say." She reached out and touched his cheek. He smiled, liking the fact that she was quoting his grandmother. Then she bolted upright, shot past him, and streaked into the bathroom, slamming the door in her wake.

Kelsey waited in the living room, darting anxious glances at the door for what seemed like a long time. Melly liked her privacy, and he didn't want to bother her. Or so he told himself. The reality was that he wasn't good with illness. Taking care of sick people required too much of him. But she was gone an inordinately long amount of time. What if she had passed out? Should he check on her?

Eventually Rocky made the decision for him. He walked to the bathroom and began anxiously pawing at the door. Kelsey followed suit. "Mel, are you decent?"

Melly gave a weak chuckle. "I guess that depends on your definition."

"I'm coming in," Kelsey declared. He pushed open the door to find Melly lying on the floor, curled into the fetal position. He left, retrieved a glass of water, and returned to crouch beside her as Rocky shoved anxiously between them. "The dog is worried about you."

"I'm fine," she said, but Kelsey wasn't sure. She looked and sounded like death. She reached over to clasp his hand. "You've seen too many weird tropical diseases and you're becoming paranoid. This is a virus. A twenty four hour thing is going around. I'm sure I'll be better tomorrow. You can go." She let go his hand and draped her arm over Rocky who was stretched out beside her as if sitting vigil.

She was probably right. She would be better tomorrow. There was nothing he could do. He should go. Instead he reached up, pulled down a clean towel, and pillowed it under his head as he lay down on the other side of Rocky.

"Kelsey," Melly began to protest.

"What kind of guy leaves his dog's mom when she's sick? Not me." He slung his arm over Rocky, resting beside hers. She laid her hand on his arm and smiled. Rocky released a loud, contented sigh and Kelsey smiled. Even though he was lying on a cold tile floor across from someone who was turning three shades of green, he felt content somehow.

"Kelsey, I missed you this weekend," Melly whispered as if confessing a horrible secret. "So much."

He thought of the woman he had tried so hard to be with, the one who looked like her, the one he had taken back to his hotel in a vain attempt to forget before kicking her out after one gut-wrenching kiss. "You have no idea," he said. He rested his hand on her bicep and gave it a reassuring squeeze.

CHAPTER 9

For the next month, Caleigh and Travis existed in a place of tacit peace. They didn't argue. Sometimes they even laughed together and had fun. Their nights were better than anything he could have hoped for or imagined. That alone should have made Travis deliriously happy. But something was missing, and he couldn't put his finger on it. Perhaps it was the subtle light in Caleigh's eyes that had never come back after his trip to Vegas. She never mentioned the weekend again, and she didn't act angry, but there was something in her demeanor that told him all was not forgiven. He was vaguely annoyed by that, but the only way to clear the air between them was to bring things to the surface and hash it all out again. And since all outward clues said she was okay, he felt crazy for looking at things that might not be there. If he asked her why her eyes didn't sparkle anymore, he would no doubt come off looking like a lunatic. So he let it go and life went on.

Perhaps the most surprising thing about marriage for Travis was how little he thought of other women and how content he felt with Caleigh. He never imagined himself settling down with one woman, at least not any time soon. He thought he would have to work at it if he ever wanted to stay faithful. But now that he was married, he found his thoughts consumed by Caleigh more often than not. With a start, he realized he was standing behind a beautiful woman one day in Starbucks and he hadn't even noticed her at first because he had been replaying a scene with Caleigh in his head. And it hadn't even been one of the good ones from the previous night, merely their mundane breakfast conversation from that morning. She got up early to eat breakfast with him before work, and he liked that, liked sharing a meal with her before he began his day. There was something peaceful and intimate about their early morning routine.

If there was one blight on their new life together, it was the fact that she hadn't found a job. As far as Travis could tell, she wasn't even looking. He didn't get it. She wasn't lazy by any means. She was always doing something, either around the house or at her parents' church. It shouldn't have been a surprise how much time she spent doing volunteer work, but it still was. Except for Gage, he had never known someone as genuinely good as Caleigh was. Her goodness evoked an odd mixture of exasperation, annoyance, and awe in him as he continually asked himself what she was doing with the likes of him. But her refusal to find work that paid was starting to become something he couldn't ignore. He believed in equality in marriage. That meant he helped with the housework—which he was willing to do, but never seemed to accomplish because it was already done by the time he arrived home. But he would have done it if she worked and needed the help. And since he was progressive on that matter, he expected her to be progressive, too. He wasn't a breadwinner. They were partners. He decided to broach the subject with her as soon as he got home and since he had tamed some of his drinking, he was fortifying himself with caffeine.

The drinking was another byproduct of marriage that took him by surprise. He hadn't intended to drink less. He didn't seem to crave it as much. And it seemed sort of ridiculous to go out and party with people he barely knew or liked while his pregnant wife stayed home alone. It was sort of funny when he thought about it. Where he had once spent his weekends getting drunk with strangers, he now spent them lying on the couch watching television while his wife played guitar or knitted. And, weirdest of all, he was happy about it. He chuckled. The beautiful woman turned to look at him with a smile. He looked away and laughed again. What was happening to him? And why did he like it?

He bought the largest and most caffeinated beverage Starbucks had to offer because he didn't simply need to talk to Caleigh about a job; he had other news to impart, and he wasn't sure how she was going to take it. When he arrived home, he found her in the living room with a few pieces of wood and some tools he didn't recognize. She looked up with a distracted smile.

"Ashleigh loaned me some of her tools. I'm going to make some shelves for the baby's room."

"Of course you are," he said. At this point nothing she did surprised him. She was a jack of all trades, fearlessly trying her hand at everything and succeeding at whatever she tried. She eyed the Starbucks drink in his hand with disapproval. Was it because he hadn't bought her one? "Want a sip?" he offered. "It's caffeinated, though." She had been ardently avoiding caffeine since she became pregnant.

"No, thanks," she said. "I would have made you something."

He shrugged one shoulder. "Theirs are better. No offense, I think it's something to do with all the fancy machines. Hard to duplicate at home."

"I suppose," she said, sounding unconvinced as she turned her attention back to the piece of wood in front of her. "They're really expensive."

On that note, he thought, taking a deep breath and a fortifying sip of espresso. "We need to talk." She looked up as he sat on the couch. She was perched on the floor but she set aside her work and moved to the couch beside him.

"What is it?" she asked.

"We received orders today. We're being deployed."

"Deployed," she repeated. "Why does that sound ominous? You guys go on assignment all the time."

"This is different. This isn't our team; we're being assigned to a platoon, not going on a mission. This is going to be a long time."

She blinked furiously a few times and cleared her throat. "Where are you going?"

"I'm not allowed to tell you," he said.

She nodded. She hated to be out of the loop, but she knew going in that most of what he did was classified. She took a steadying breath and asked the question that meant the most. "Will you be back in time for the baby?"

"I don't know. The assignment is open-ended. That means there's no set return date. This assignment is Nick's baby; he's going to be in charge of the whole platoon. We're along for the ride. So blame him if you want to be mad at someone." He was only half kidding. He knew how much she wanted him to be there for the baby's birth.

"I'm not mad," she assured him. She looked fragile, diminished somehow. He wasn't great at knowing what to do with her, but even he could see she needed comfort. He set aside his coffee and took her in his arms. She melted into him, pressing the barely-there bulge of her stomach against him. His hand went there automatically and he stifled his own disappointment. Though he hadn't given it as much thought as she had, he had been looking forward to seeing his kid brought into the world. Things weren't looking good for that now. The baby was due in four months. Travis had the feeling this deployment would take six or maybe more.

Her face pressed to his neck, and he could feel her suppressing tears. It was odd to have someone who cared when he went away. Gage cared, of course, but he was military himself so he understood. To have a woman who would miss him, who depended on his return, was something altogether different. It touched a part of him that hadn't been exposed since his mother died.

"I'll be okay," Caleigh said, her voice hoarse and raw. "You don't have to worry about us while you're gone. We'll be fine."

"I know you will," he said, smiling. "You can do anything, Caleigh. I've never known anyone like you."

She smiled against him. Her cheeks felt warm and he wondered if she was blushing. The moment was perfect and beautiful so of course he had to ruin it. "It will help pass the time when you get a job," he said. She stiffened in his embrace before pulling away to look at him.

"What do you mean?"

"What do you mean what do I mean? A job. Work."

"I'm not going to work," she said.

Not only was she serious, but she sounded offended. "What are you talking about? Everyone works."

"My mom doesn't. She stayed at home with us."

"That was like a million years ago, Caleigh. We can't afford that."

"We can," she said.

"We can't," he said.

"We can. Don't use that patronizing tone with me like I'm an idiot. I know how much you make, and I know how much it takes to live. In fact, there's something I've been meaning to talk to you about. I think we should trade in the truck."

"What?" he practically yelled. His truck was a sacred cow, the first thing he had bought when he started making money.

"It's totally impractical. It has two doors, no back seat, and the payment is ridiculously expensive. I've been making some calls. We could get a family car that gets better mileage and costs a couple hundred dollars less a month, to say nothing of the drop in insurance rates."

He blinked at her in shock. She had made calls about trading in his truck? It was his truck. "Or you could get a job and we could buy a second car."

"We don't need a second car when you're out of the country half the time."

"So, what, you're going to loaf around and sponge off me forever?" he asked.

"No, I'm going to raise your child and manage your house."

"What's to manage? We have three rooms."

She dashed to her feet, hands on hips. "Do you even know what you're saying? Who's going to watch the baby while I work?"

"Uh, a babysitter," he suggested in a tone that told her exactly what he thought of her logic.

"And do you know how much babysitters cost? A lot, probably almost as much as I would make from any job. Not to mention the fact that a stranger would be watching our child. I'm not an idiot, Travis. I'm good with money, and I've run the numbers. We can make it on one salary if we cut back a little. That means trading in your monstrosity of a truck, a truck that screams you're a bachelor without a family, and cutting back on extras like that five dollar latte." She pointed to his drink as if it were a vat of poison.

He searched his brain for a retort, trying to think of some extravagance for which he could accuse her, but there was none. As far as he could tell, Caleigh never bought anything, which was another strike against her. Why did she have to be so ever-loving good and conscientious all the time? He stood, needing the height advantage. "I am not getting rid of my truck. And you are exaggerating about the money. We can't make it on my salary—*I* could barely make it on my salary."

"That's because you're horrible with money," she yelled. "You had nothing in savings. I brought five thousand dollars into this marriage, and I've managed to save a thousand more since we've been married."

That stopped him again. They had six thousand dollars in the bank? That was more than he'd ever had in his life. He glanced toward the television, wondering how much it would cost to upgrade—a tactical error because Caleigh guessed the direction of his thoughts.

"You are not a kid anymore," she yelled. "It's not about you, or your truck, or your video games, or your television, or premium cable. It's about our family and your child. Grow up and be a man, Travis."

She went too far. If there was one thing Travis couldn't stand, it was being told what to do. "Why don't you grow up, Caleigh? Time to stop living in fantasy land. We are not your parents, as much as you want to make us so. Ashleigh works. Why can't you? Are you too good for it? Get a job, little girl, and stop pretending we're Ward and June Cleaver."

"How could I do that?" she yelled. "Ward never left June to go to a nudie club. You want to pretend you're still single, but you're not. You have responsibilities now."

"Responsibilities I never wanted, never asked for." He could feel himself teetering toward the edge and knew he should pull back, but restraint had never been his specialty, so he dived over the edge. "I never wanted you, I never wanted this, I never wanted the baby." He pointed to her stomach. The silence hung between them like a physical presence as the color washed from Caleigh's face. She picked up his keys and left the house. He stood still, debating about whether or not he should go after her. He had gone too far, and even he knew it.

The truck started and idled a few minutes before she came back inside. "I have nowhere else to go," she said. She sounded defeated, broken. He reached out, but she bypassed him and went into the baby's room, closing and locking the door once she was safely inside.

CHAPTER 10

The following week was busy for Travis with briefings and meetings back to back. Nick was now not only their team leader, he was in charge of the whole platoon. Their entire team had received a promotion. Nick was moved to First Lieutenant which meant Kelsey advanced to sergeant, Truck became a corporal, and Travis was promoted to Lance Corporal. His new title came with a pay increase, as did his deployment. The extra money ensured Caleigh really didn't have to get a job. He told her about the pay raises with no small amount of swallowed pride, but she took it in stride, remaining quiet as she had been since their fight.

Their new assignment was not only going to be longer than usual, but it was a green operation instead of a black op. Travis was trying not to feel resentful about that, but he had joined the team because of the black ops. He liked tracking down the bad guys and taking them out. They were like surgeons removing decaying or diseased flesh by cutting it out, swift and clean. Now they were doing recon with no payoff, at least not for them. They would spend the next few months laying sensors and gathering intel that may or may not lead to further action. There was some danger involved in the work because, like always, they were going to be somewhere they weren't supposed to be. But this assignment lacked the same panache as being part of a scout sniper team. This was drudge work done by a larger group of men who would all have to find some way to entertain themselves in the middle of nowhere for the foreseeable future.

There was one thing the team had to do before they deployed, however, and Travis was roped into helping out.

"Why do I have to wear this?" he asked, looking down at the white sheet that had been made into a toga-style robe.

"It's important for your character to stay authentic," Kelsey replied.

"There's really no reason beyond you wanting to see me in this, is there?" Travis asked.

"I've been plotting this moment since you joined the team. Don't ruin this for me." Kelsey gave him a little shove and sent him on his way. Travis's only consolation was that they were off base, but there was no doubt word would spread. He saw Shelby from a distance. He didn't mean to sneak up on her, but so much time spent in Special Forces had made him a stalker by nature. She jumped and flinched when he reached her, at least until she took in his ridiculous getup. Apparently there was a reason for the costume because no one looking at him could ever take him as a threat. After Shelby's initial reaction, she laughed. They were all careful with her, even Travis who hadn't been privy to her horrible ordeal. He was almost glad Kelsey had dressed him in the stupid costume if it put her so readily at ease.

"What's up, Travis?" she asked. Her puzzled tone told him she didn't have a clue about why he was there, dressed like a frat boy on hiatus. He pulled out the scroll Kelsey had given him and pretended to read.

"Shelby Lance, tonight you will be visited by three ghosts of marine deployments. At the end of the evening, you will be given the chance to change your life forever. Take heed you make the right choice." He studied her surreptitiously as he rolled the scroll. Her face was flushed with excitement, her eyes bright with repressed hope that he meant what she thought he meant. The expression caused him to feel a little sad and wistful. Caleigh had been robbed of the courting process. His proposal had consisted of a ring and the ubiquitous "Will you marry me?" He hadn't put thought, time, or effort into making it something she would have enjoyed.

She should have put up more of a fuss. She should have complained over what a loser I am in the romance department. But she hadn't, like she hadn't mentioned a word about the painful things he had hurled at her a few days ago. Instead she had bottled up all her hurt and soldiered on. The old, familiar anger rose to the surface again, making him realize it had been oddly absent since his marriage. He gave Shelby a cursory nod and walked away before he could explode at her for something that wasn't her fault. He wanted, no, needed a release for this pent up rage. Why did everything have to be wrong? He had never wanted to marry Caleigh and now that he had he was upset because it wasn't going well. His emotions were muddled and complex, adding to his anger. Life was simpler when he was anesthetized.

With that thought came the answer he was looking for. He hadn't gotten drunk in way too long. What was he waiting for? He hopped in his truck, drove to his favorite bar, and allowed himself to forget everything.

Meanwhile the other members of his team, Ashleigh, Melly, and a handful of uncredited players, got down to business. The need for haste had caused Kelsey to seek outside help to pull off Truck's proposal before they deployed. In the mayhem of trying to get everything ready in time for the big event, no one noticed Travis's absence —no one but Caleigh. She had thought, or rather hoped, he was looking forward to the upcoming event as much as she was, but apparently not because he was nowhere to be found. She guessed where he was. There was a not-so-small part of her that wanted to tattle to Kelsey or Nick and have one of them retrieve him, but she didn't. Not only because it wasn't their place to parent her husband, but because she was too embarrassed to admit defeat. She was an idiot, but at least she could be an idiot with a shred of pride.

Later that night as Shelby pretended to sleep, Kelsey stole into her room. With anyone else, they wouldn't have given her advance notice of the adventure. But she had been through too much trauma to take any chances. When he opened her bedroom door, she was sitting up smiling at him in anticipation.

"I am the ghost of deployments past," he announced. "Come with me if you want to live." He held out his hand and she took it, following him from the room.

"We're stopping in the living room?" she asked, sounding a little disappointed.

"No, we're starting in the living room. I thought you would complain less than Scrooge; don't prove me wrong."

She stifled a laugh and clasped her hands behind her back, waiting.

"Shelby, Shelby, Shelby," Kelsey said, shaking his head in disapproval. "You spent the first part of your life away from the marines, never having eaten an MRE, your ears undamaged by the report of gunfire, always living in the same place, always knowing where you were going to be in a few months. I weep for you, I really do. Let us pause and reflect on your life." He pushed the play button on the DVD player and Shelby's parents appeared on the screen. It had taken a bit of arranging to get the footage, but Kelsey was nothing if not resourceful. An airman who owed him a favor drove from the Air Force base in Lackland to Shelby's parents—still a four hour drive because Texas was huge. Her parents were game for the idea, though, and got into the spirit of things, making Shelby's history seem like a tragedy because they hadn't been a military family.

Her brother and sisters took turns lamenting the fact that they had to shop at regular stores instead of a commissary or Navy Exchange Store. Kelsey had sent them a list of talking points, but they improvised to the point of hyperbole. He had the feeling he would like them if he ever met them. By the end of the video, Shelby was laughing while wiping a few tears for the family so far away.

"Think on these things, Shelby Whatsits," Kelsey said, using the nickname he had given her when they first met. "It's not too late to change your sad, military-free life." He eased out of the room and Nick took his place in his Battle Dress Gear, sans gun or sword.

"I am the ghost of deployments present, Shelby," Nick said. "I have a sad tale to impart, if you think you're ready."

"I'm ready," Shelby said, her grave tone and somber expression trying and failing to match his when she smiled quickly before wiping it away.

"Let's go, then," Nick said. He held out his arm to her, and she took his elbow. They walked to his car and he drove her to the base. As he led her to the barracks, he started to talk again. "We're about to see the sad tale of Tiny Tim Stokes, a marine with no one to love. It's very sad. I hope you can handle it."

Though it was almost the middle of the night, the barracks were blazing and buzzing with activity as if it were the middle of the day. It was also decorated to look like the desert with camo and strategically-placed MRE's, weapons, and gear.

"Mail call," a private announced as he set a large box on the table. A handful of marines in battle dress descended on it and began sorting the packages. One lone private hovered in the background. "Anything for me?" he asked, blatant hope and longing in his tone. Everyone ignored him as they loudly exclaimed over their packages.

"A letter from my wife!" one called, holding it aloft.

"My daughters drew me a picture," another said.

"My fiancée sent cookies!"

"Is there anything for Stokes?" Stokes tried again. "Tiny Tim Stokes? Anything?"

At last the private who made the mail call turned his attention to Stokes. "I'm afraid not, Stokes. That's all there was. There's nothing, nothing for you. If only you had a girl of your very own to love you." He hung his head, shaking it in sadness as he picked up the empty box and walked from the room. Stokes walked to a bunk and sat, dropping his head to his hands as he pretended to cry.

"Poor Tiny Tim Stokes," Nick said.

Shelby chortled a laugh because "Tiny" Tim Stokes was huge. In camo paint he probably looked like the Hulk. Nick gave her a reproachful look for laughing and she bit her lip.

"If only he had somebody to love, if only there was some woman willing to join her life to his and save him from his lonely fate. It's too late for him, but perhaps there is another whose fate is yet undetermined. Let's go." He took her elbow and led her from the barracks. This time they drove to the beach. As soon as they lit from the car, Shelby could see the lights. There appeared to be thousands of white candles, flickering madly in the ocean breeze. The bass's jazz band was playing and Kelsey had somehow procured a fog machine so when Ashton stepped forward it looked like he appeared from mist.

"I am the ghost of deployments future," he said. He was wearing his dress uniform and holding a dozen white roses. He stopped short in front of her and handed them over. "Tonight you've witnessed the sad state of your life without the marines, and you've seen the sad state of the marines without you. Tell me, Shelby Lance, are you ready to change your civilian ways?"

"What did you have in mind, marine?" she asked.

"We met in the sand so I thought it was only appropriate we have this conversation in the sand, too, Shelby. You've seen the true story of what my life is like. It's not always going to be easy or fun. It's risky. It's maddening. But it's nothing without you. So what I'm about to ask doesn't concern only me. I come with a team and a battalion." He got down on one knee and pulled out a ring. "When you marry a marine, you marry the corps. I guess what I'm asking is will you marry us?" From the shadows the other members of the platoon started to appear. All of them were waiting silently, breathlessly for Shelby's answer.

"One condition," Shelby said.

"What?" Ashton asked. He sounded wary—he hadn't been prepared for conditions.

"You're the only one allowed on our honeymoon."

"Don't do it," one of the marines yelled.

Ashton waved him away. "Deal," he said.

"Then yes, I'll marry you," Shelby agreed. There was an ear-splitting "Oorah!" from the surrounding marines, so loud it temporarily drowned out the roar of the ocean. Caleigh watched as Ashton slipped the ring on Shelby's finger before standing to kiss her. She tried not to let her own jealousy tamp down the joy she felt for her friends. She was genuinely happy for them; she loved them both and wished them only the best. But there was a small part of her that almost resented their happiness. What would it be like to be loved and wanted so much?

On her left side, Nick edged close to Ashleigh and kissed her as they no doubt were reliving their own glorious romance. On her right side, Melly and Kelsey studiously avoided eye contact with each other. Instead Melly and Caleigh caught each other's eye and shared a sympathetic smile. For this moment they were soul sisters—both left out of the love fest. Melly couldn't seem to get it together with Kelsey and Caleigh's husband was off getting drunk somewhere alone, or worse, not alone. She could only hope he would come home alone. She thought he had been faithful since their marriage—if one didn't count Vegas as infidelity—but she had no idea if that would change when he drank. After all, he had been half buzzed when he got her pregnant. If he had been thinking clearly, he never would have done it. He had made that sentiment more than clear the other night. Why he married her was a mystery. He must love his career a whole lot to be willing to subject himself to something so horrible.

She was thoroughly drenched in self-pity by the time Kelsey offered to take her home. "Where's Mr. Caleigh?" he asked as he led her to his truck, his arm draped over her shoulders. Caleigh was thankful for whatever providence kept her from being attracted to him. Kelsey was a lady killer with his boyish charm and drop-dead good looks. As it was, she had only ever seen him in a brotherly light, and the feeling appeared to be mutual. She was definitely the little sister he never had.

"I can only wonder," she said. He opened the passenger door and lifted her into the high seat. When he was finished, he didn't move away.

"You doing okay, kiddo?"

It was on the tip of her tongue to tell him everything, to pour out her misery and stupidity, but something held her back. Maybe it was her newly gained maturity, or maybe it was pride. Either way, she forced a smile and shook her head. "Are you deflecting? Cause you look a little down in the mouth yourself, kiddo." She patted his cheek.

He smiled, but his tone was serious when he answered. "Did you ever think life should come with a manual to tell us how to stop screwing it up all the time?"

"Every minute lately," Caleigh said.

"I guess we'll keep on keeping on together," Kelsey said.

"That's what family is for," Caleigh agreed.

"See? Exactly. And you don't need a ring to realize we are family." His eyebrows slammed together in frustration.

She held up her left hand with a self-deprecating smile. "I already have a ring. Believe me when I tell you sometimes it means nothing at all."

"You want me to kill him for you? Cause I will," Kelsey offered.

"Maybe later," Caleigh said.

"Say the word, the offer is open." He closed her door and jogged to his side. They arrived at her house, finding it empty. Kelsey saw her inside and locked up, checking the windows, too. He was being thoughtful, but for Caleigh it was another blow, another reminder of what she was missing with Travis.

When Travis stumbled home at three in the morning, he didn't check the locks; he barely remembered to close the door. And when he fell into bed, he didn't realize his wife wasn't there. Not until the next morning did he find her sleeping soundly on the floor of their baby's room, curled in a ball, her cheeks puffy from unshed tears.

CHAPTER 11

The team and their platoon deployed three days later. Travis and Caleigh had regressed back to a place of mutual denial. Both acknowledged the major issues between them, but neither felt they could be fixed in the short time before Travis left the country. Not that either of them believed their issues could be fixed when Travis returned, but at least it was better to spend their final hours together in peace rather than arguing. For those three days, they slipped into the comfortable pattern of their first couple of weeks of marriage with Travis going to work and coming home to a clean house and a nice dinner, like any happily married couple. For seventy two hours they could pretend to be anything.

The big day arrived and Caleigh felt queasy. In theory, she was ready for deployments. But theory and reality were often at odds. She had said goodbye to Lolly once in this same fashion, standing at the airport while he hugged her and kissed her cheeks. She had waved cheerfully as she watched his plane ascend and then he never came home again. Now she was saying goodbye to another marine, this time on a boat. This marine was her husband, the father of her unborn child. How much worse would the pain be if something happened to him?

Travis was feeling his own uncertainty about going away. It was different to go on a mission when the only person left behind was Gage. Now he had Caleigh and their baby depending on him to return. Staying alive had never seemed so important, his future never so uncertain. True, they were going on a green op, but green ops could go wrong as easily as a black op. Or their plane could go down. There were a million different things that could go wrong, things he had never thought about before because he hadn't cared if he lived or died. Now he cared, if only to make sure his wife and child were taken care of. It was an odd feeling, this new protectiveness. Travis wasn't at all sure he liked it.

Caleigh's legs felt weak when Travis picked her up and crushed her to him in a toe-curling kiss. Her feet dangled off the floor while he pressed his face to her neck. "If you need anything, tell me and I'll make sure you get it," he said. They were going to be off the grid with a few scheduled times to communicate. He wouldn't be totally cut off from her.

"I'll be fine," she assured him.

"I know you will," he said. He let her go and rested his hands on her shoulders. "You can do anything, Caleigh. You're capable and good at everything." He paused, swallowing hard. "I'm sorry for the things I said."

"Forget it," Caleigh said. "Take care of you." She swallowed down a lump of panic and clung, burying her face against him so he wouldn't see her fear. Reluctantly, he let her go and moved away, embarking the boat as Caleigh fought another wave of nausea.

Gage was there. He slipped his arm around her and gave her shoulders a squeeze. She leaned into him more than she normally would have, hating herself for feeling so weak.

On Gage's other side, Melly was doing her best not to cling to Kelsey. He framed her face with his hands. "Take care of my dog. I love that dog," he said.

"The dog loves you, too," she replied. They smiled because neither of them was really talking about the dog. He let her go and stood back, waiting for Nick and Ashton to finish their goodbyes to Ashleigh and Shelby and then they walked the plank together.

Gage reached out and offered his other arm to Melly. She moved close and leaned into him, smiling. Gage looked down and caught sight of Caleigh looking pale and shaky. "Always send him off with a smile," he whispered. "There will be time for tears later."

She was afraid to open her mouth, afraid to try and tell him she wasn't afraid of crying; she was afraid of losing her breakfast or worse. Their men stood on the deck while the boat began its departure. The women waved madly, blowing kisses and trying hard not to cry.

Kelsey stood beside Travis, watching the scene below. This departure felt different. For as long as he had been a sniper, his assignments had been short. He had grown used to the revolving door his life had become. Going away for months felt more than a little lonely. Beside him, his teammates seemed to be feeling the same thing. Their usual zest for a mission was missing. Kelsey's eyes landed on Gage or, more specifically, Gage's arm where it lay on Melly's body. He wanted to rip it off and throw it in the ocean.

"Aren't we lucky to have your brother, the superhero, to look after our women?" Kelsey asked Travis, more than a hint of sarcasm and anger in his tone.

"Sure thing," Travis said with his own heavy dose of resentment. Gage had promised to be present for the birth of his baby, as if that was any consolation to Travis who would miss it all.

"That your wife, Vega?"

Travis's head inclined over his shoulder to see a marine he knew by name only, Lance Corporal Clint Hanlan. "Is there a reason you're asking?"

"I wouldn't kick her out of my room, you know what I'm saying?" Hanlan said, leering to make sure Travis knew exactly what he was saying.

Travis reviewed his options. He could give in to his baser instincts and tear Hanlan apart, thereby buying himself a one way ticket off the boat. That option was tempting. Instinct told him that was what Hanlan wanted, however. Why seek out the most volatile guy on the mission unless it was on purpose? Option two, he could wait and see how things developed. "I thought the same thing about your mom," Travis replied.

Now it was Hanlan who looked like his control snapped. He took a step forward as Kelsey leaned down and spoke. "Why are we whispering? No fair keeping secrets."

Hanlan paused, glancing at the stripes on Kelsey's arm. "Forget it, Sergeant. It was nothing." Before he turned away, he flashed Travis a look that said it wasn't nothing and he definitely didn't intend to forget it.

Kelsey and Travis watched him walk away. "Look at you, already making friends with the other kids on your first day of kindergarten," Kelsey said.

"I've always been a people person," Travis said.

"Seriously, what was that about?" Kelsey asked.

"No idea," Travis replied.

"It's like you have a sign on your forehead that says 'Trouble, please find me,'" Kelsey said.

"It's a gift," Travis agreed.

Kelsey leaned close again, speaking in a low tone that no longer sounded friendly. "This is Nick's first command. Nick, your team leader, brother-in-law, and all around good guy. I swear if you do anything to mess this up the way you mess up everything, I will personally see to it that you spend the remainder of your career peeling potatoes in northern Alaska."

"Aye, Sergeant," Travis said with a salute that, though technically correct, was still loaded with sarcasm.

"Your wife is a saint," Kelsey added.

"At least I have one," Travis said.

Kelsey turned back toward the horizon. "It's going to be a long six months."

Travis didn't reply, but he couldn't have agreed more.

* * *

ON THE SHORE, their family and friends were having their own bit of drama. Rocky, startled by the sound of the boat as it moved from the dock, broke free of Melly and dashed away. When he realized the humans were chasing him, he thought they were playing a fun game and began a mad dash, weaving in and out of people whose tears turned to laughter when they caught sight of the dog. Melly, Gage, Ashleigh, Shelby, and Reverend and Mrs. Desmond all gave chase until seemingly everyone on the dock was running, laughing, screaming or barking. Everyone except Caleigh. She remained rooted to the spot, the watery smile still welded on her face.

It was Gage who first noticed that she wasn't partaking in their dog-chasing adventure. It was also he who caught Rocky and brought him back to submission. He was heading toward Melly's car when he stopped short, realizing Caleigh wasn't with their party. When he turned and saw her standing by herself at the edge of the crowd, he felt a flicker of annoyance. She was never going to make it as a military wife if she turned into a cream puff at the first deployment.

Thinking he would give her a friendly pep talk, he handed Rocky over to his owner and went to retrieve Caleigh. "Hey," he said, aiming for cheerfulness and not reproof. She was a kid, after all. "The first goodbye is always the hardest, but it gets easier."

"Gage, I don't think…" her hand raised shakily to his arm. "I don't feel…" And then she dropped. If not for his quick reflexes, she would have smacked hard on the pavement. As it was, he deftly caught her, lifting her as he sprinted to his car.

AS GAGE PROMISED TRAVIS, he was present for the birth of the baby, hovering anxiously in the hallway, pacing back and forth like a 1950's father who had been excommunicated from the mother's room. Only Ashleigh was beside Caleigh as she pushed her too small, too still baby into the world. Soon after, they gave Caleigh something to knock her out, to take away the pain. But there had been no pain, at least not physically. Her baby was so small he required only one push to arrive unmoving into the universe. The pain was deeper and in places the drugs couldn't reach.

When she woke, the room was so silent and still she thought she was alone. So it was with a start that she realized she wasn't. Her father-in-law, the Admiral, sat silently beside her bed, looking uncomfortable and out of place.

"Hello, Caleigh," he said. "Is there anything I can get you?"

"No, thank you," she replied. She was confused, not only by the haze of drugs, but by the appearance of the man she least expected to see, especially because he looked like he would rather be anywhere else.

He shifted, leaning forward to clasp his hands together. "I'm not sure the impression my son has given you. I simply wanted to say our family takes care of its own. If you need anything…" he trailed off. "I've never been good with, uh, emotional things." He paused, let go his hands, and tugged his collar. "I suppose what I'm trying to say is I'm sorry this happened and I, um, am here for…anything." He paused before blurting again, "Do you need money?"

If Caleigh didn't know Travis, she might think the Admiral was being callous or trying to buy her off. As it was, she recognized where Travis inherited his inability to say the right thing at the right time, so she mustered a smile. "I'm fine, thank you."

The Admiral nodded. "Right, then. I won't linger. There's work and you don't need me here fussing and making things uncomfortable." After another forced smile, he stood, preparing to make his escape. Caleigh caught his arm and he looked at it in surprise as if it didn't belong to him.

"Thank you for coming. I know you're very busy. It means a lot to me that you came."

He nodded again, giving her hand a pat where it lay on his forearm. She watched him walk out of the room as Gage took his place, almost like a prearranged tag team. "Your family is in the waiting room," Gage said in answer to Caleigh's unasked question. Her family wasn't the type to be absent during an emergency. They were more likely to be hovering, stifling Caleigh with their desire to take away her pain. Frankly, she was glad for the reprieve.

"I have to get back to Charleston," Gage added. "I wanted to make sure and reiterate what Dad said. If you need anything, Caleigh, anything at all, then ask and it's yours. Money or…" he trailed off, unable to think of anything else she might need.

They must know Travis's proclivity to spend whatever he earns as soon as he earns it, Caleigh thought. For some reason she was irritated by the assumption she and Travis were in dire financial straits, especially when it wasn't true. "We're doing fine," she assured him.

Gage blinked at her, clearly disbelieving. "I'm glad to hear that, but we're family, so don't hesitate to ask for anything."

"There is something I want," Caleigh said. She hastened to finish when he made a move toward his wallet. "I don't want Travis to know about the baby. No one has tried to contact him yet, have they?"

"Of course not. They won't be within range for a few more days," Gage said. "But are you sure this is the kind of thing you want to keep from him? I think he should know."

She shook her head. "He has enough to worry about without adding issues from home. And isn't it the military wife's mission to handle everything while the soldier is away? I'm pretty sure I read somewhere once that we're never supposed to burden them with problems from home."

"Not this, though," Gage said. "He would want to know. You need the emotional support."

There was no way to explain to him the best emotional support would come from Travis not knowing about the baby. There was too much chance he'd be relieved. If he was, if she sensed his relief over the death of their child, then she would never be able to forgive him. What she told Gage was true, too. There was nothing Travis could do from so far away other than commiserate. But why would he commiserate over a baby he had never wanted? No, it was better for all concerned if Caleigh handled it on her own and broke the news to Travis later. Maybe by then she would be better able to handle his reaction.

Sensing her resolve, Gage capitulated. "All right, I'll spread the word. Travis isn't to know. If you change your mind, and I think you should, then I can talk to him if you want." He patted her arm, gave her one more reassuring smile, and left the room. Caleigh shouldn't have found the ensuing silence so comfortable, but she did, at least for the next sixty seconds until her family arrived, pouring sympathy on her wounds, trying their level best to take away the hurt.

Even though she was half out of it, Caleigh couldn't fail to see the irony in the situation. Her family had spent her life trying to save her from pain. For all of that time, she had resented their interference. Yet now when she actually wanted them to save her, they couldn't; the pain ran too deep for saving. They were standing right next to her, talking, touching, soothing, but she felt a thousand miles away, adrift in a sea of her own despair. At last when it became too much she closed her eyes, cutting them off by finding solace in sleep.

CHAPTER 12

Two months later, Caleigh was still sleeping. Occasionally she woke to eat and drink, but only when her family insisted on it. They showed up every day, reminding her to shower, take care of her personal needs, and oversee her finances. Ashleigh asked her to move in with her for the duration of the deployment, and their parents wanted the same thing. Caleigh put them off by saying nothing at all. Arguing would have taken too much energy; silence was easier.

One day there was a knock she didn't recognize. Her family didn't knock, so she knew it wasn't them. She listened to make sure whoever it was went away. Surely no salesman on the planet was persistent enough to wait her out. But apparently one was because the knocking wouldn't cease. After ten solid minutes of incessant pounding, Caleigh dragged herself from her bed to answer, blinking in confusion not only at the streaming sunlight but at her brother-in-law.

"You look like a yellow rose type of girl," he said, handing her a large bouquet. "Actually, you look like a daffodil type of girl, but they're out of season. Roses had to do." He eased passed her and headed toward the kitchen. Caleigh stood staring blankly at the flowers in her hand a few seconds before stumbling behind him.

"Did I know you were coming?" she asked.

"Not unless you're psychic," he said. He opened the refrigerator and frowned at the contents.

"My family keeps me well stocked," Caleigh noted. The fridge was stuffed to capacity.

"None of this food has been eaten," Gage said.

"I eat," Caleigh protested. "Some," she added when he scanned her with a critical eye. "Do you want something? I could put something together." Even as she made the offer, she hoped he would say no. Eyeing the chair, she eased close to the table and slunk down, resting her head on the cool oak surface.

Gage took one of Travis's beers—one that her father must have miraculously missed during his prohibition-type purge—and flipped it open. He sat down beside her and took a long draw.

"I didn't know you drank," Caleigh noted, not caring one way or the other. Conversation seemed to be important, though, so she had to say something.

"I don't much. Only when I'm upset about something."

"Did you and Melly have a fight?" she asked. She closed her eyes. Why wouldn't he leave? Couldn't he see she wasn't up for any family bonding time? Her own family was due to arrive for their daily checkup. Why couldn't everyone leave her alone?

"I'm upset about you," he snapped.

Caleigh's eyes flicked open. "Travis said you never get angry," she said.

"Travis is wrong about a lot of things. Look, Caleigh, you're my little brother's wife and, more than that, I like you. You're a sweet kid and a good person. Everyone is worried about you. I'm the ringer sent in to try and make a last ditch effort to try and wake you up. As we both know, I never fail at anything." He paused to bestow a self-deprecating smile. "So here's what we're going to do: You're going to get dressed and come out with me and Melly tonight."

"I don't feel very social right now."

"I wasn't asking; I was telling. You have ten minutes to dress, or you're going in your pajamas."

She bit her lip, trying to decide if he was serious. Her eyes rested on the beer. "It seems so easy for other people to drown their sorrows. I've never tasted beer."

He hugged the bottle closer to his chest. "You're not starting now. There's something seriously wrong with the system when you're old enough to marry before you're old enough to drink. I'm not an enabler, and I'm not going to lose my career for providing alcohol to a minor. You have nine minutes."

Reluctantly, she shrugged away from the table and threw on the first clothes she found. She had no idea what the weather was like since she hadn't set foot outside her house in eight weeks. It was bright, that much she knew—much, much too bright. She gathered her sunglasses when she shuffled back to the kitchen. Gage didn't comment on her appearance. Caleigh didn't care enough to wonder if that was a good or bad sign. He stood and herded her toward the door before thinking better of it, returning to the kitchen, and plucking a single rose from the bouquet.

"Gotta have one for my girl. Don't tell her about the other eleven," he said.

Her brow puckered at hearing Melly described as his girl. Caleigh thought of Melly as Kelsey's girl. But Gage was her brother-in-law and she liked him. Shouldn't she be happy about them? This was more than she had thought about anything in a long time, and it was too much. Whomever Melly was with, it really wasn't any of Caleigh's concern. She hoped her friend was happy, though in her darkened state it was difficult to imagine anyone being happy. She felt cynical— an emotion she had never experienced before her marriage.

"You don't think Melly's going to mind you bringing a third wheel tonight?" she asked.

"Would I be with the type of woman who would mind my tagalong kid sister-in-law? The answer is no. Besides, Melly is chairperson of the 'Save Caleigh Committee.' Believe me when I tell you she'll be thrilled to see you." He held the passenger door of his cute little convertible. "Talked to Travis lately?" he asked after he slid behind the wheel and put on his own sunglasses. They were reflective aviators and she found herself smiling. He was almost too cool to be real sometimes.

"Communication has been spotty. Why are you dating Melly?" She was suddenly insatiably curious about that. He was almost but not quite as handsome as Kelsey and seemed a thousand times more settled and mature. Why was he driving four hours to date a woman he met at a wedding?

"Sometimes what you're looking for turns up in unusual places," he said. When she was beginning to think he was a die-hard romantic, he spoiled the notion. "Plus I've dated everyone in Charleston. Branching out was a necessity." He glanced at her with a smile. She saw her reflection in his glasses and her smile died. No doubt about it, she was a mess. She tried to finger comb her hair as she turned toward her window. Maybe Melly could loan her some lip gloss and mascara so she didn't look like such a zombie.

"Do you really want to get married and settle down?" she asked. "You're only twenty seven."

"Says the nineteen-year-old child bride," he said.

"I'm a cautionary tale now," she said, her temporary levity sucked away as with the tide.

"Caleigh, this is going to sound cliché, but things will get better."

"Will they, Gage?" she asked. "Because I can't see how." Her eyes filled with tears as she thought of the few lackluster conversations she'd shared with Travis. To his credit, he was making an effort to sound like he missed her. But he hadn't asked about the baby. Not once. And if he noted that his wife had been replaced by a soulless robot who didn't comb her hair, he didn't comment on it.

They arrived at Melly's house, but neither made a move to leave the car. "After my mom died, I thought my world was over," Gage said. "For a while it was. But time has a way of forcing you to move on and heal, even when you don't want to sometimes. The pain is still there, but it's livable. You start to function again, you start to feel without every breath being agony. So, yes, Caleigh, things will get better. Believe me. But it's not going to happen holed up in your house. You have people who are dying to care about you. Let them."

It was on the tip of her tongue to explode at him, to tell him he couldn't possibly understand how she felt. But she had never been one to punish others with her pain and anger and she wasn't about to start now. Gage was trying to take care of her in the best way he knew how and she appreciated it. He might not be her brother-in-law much longer, which made the moment even more poignant. "I'll try," she whispered.

"That's all any of us can ask from you," he said. He sniffed, turning his attention toward the house. "I can smell the peppers from out here. A woman who cooks, Caleigh." He thumped his hand over his heart a couple of times. "Gets me every time. C'mon."

She followed him to the house where she was greeted by a set of giant paws that landed on her shoulders. "Whoa, Melly, this dog is huge!" The dog stared her in the face, sizing her up, and she couldn't help but laugh. His serious expression was in direct contrast to his floppy ears and awkwardly large size.

"I know," Melly said in a tone usually reserved for mothers talking about their beloved children. "Isn't he the best?"

"He's pretty great," Caleigh admitted. She petted Rocky, knuckling under his ear as his sighed in blissful contentment. "I think my shoulders are breaking, though. How do you get him down?"

"Rocky, down," Melly called. Reluctantly he dropped his paws and obeyed, giving Caleigh an adoring look that told her their bonding session was far from over. She found herself smiling again, an action that was now so rare it felt odd on her face. She dropped to her knees and he gleefully trotted back, rubbing his head against her shoulder so she had to grab the edge of the table to keep from being bowled over. She pressed her face to his neck and felt a wave of endorphins. *I've missed being happy,* she thought as her fingers sleeked over his fur. The moment was fleeting, but it was enough to remind her life hadn't always been hard. Maybe someday it would cease to be so dreary once more.

From her vantage point on the floor, she observed Melly and Gage as they interacted with each other. For the last few weeks, she had been out of the loop, not caring about anything at all. It was with some surprise she found herself curious about their relationship now. Were they in love? Was this the real deal?

There was a lot of cute banter typical of many couples in the early dating stages, but beyond that Caleigh couldn't get a read on them. They didn't seem overly affectionate with each other, but she was there so maybe they were being reserved for her benefit. Gage had kissed her when he first arrived, but it had been a perfunctory peck on the lips which was also Kelsey's typical greeting for Melly these days. All of a sudden Caleigh wished Gage gone so she could have a chat session with Melly and find out what the story was. Not that Melly would necessarily tell her. She wasn't one for wearing her heart on her sleeve. Most of the time it was anyone's guess but Kelsey's what she was thinking. He was either the only one with an inside track or the only one bold enough to pry.

"Have you heard your sister's latest scheme?" Melly asked her.

"Not that I remember," Caleigh said, frowning. Ashleigh talked to her every day. Didn't mean she listened or remembered what was said.

"She's renovating her kitchen, and she's recruited us to help."

"Us?" Caleigh repeated.

"Us, you, me, Shelby, and all the other platoon member's wives and girlfriends. She's decided to teach us all how to function when the men are away, sort of like a crash course in construction and home repair. The other women are really excited about it. They're making t-shirts. Guess what they're calling themselves?"

"What?" Caleigh asked.

"Force Reconstruction," she said, smiling. It was a play on Force Reconnaissance, or Force Recon, the term used for marines in special forces.

Caleigh laughed and shook her head. Her sister was irrepressible. Ashleigh probably felt it was her duty to lead the women of her husband's platoon while he led the men. If she had lost a baby, she would no doubt have left the hospital and started building cribs for children in need. No way would she become a worthless recluse.

Tears clouded her eyes and she blinked them away. "Are you going to do it?"

"I don't know," Melly said, her smile slipping. "I'm not really connected anymore. I'm afraid I would feel out of place."

"Melly, once a marine always a marine. You lost a brother in battle. Your place there is set for life," Caleigh said.

"Are you going to do it?" Melly asked.

Caleigh bit her lip. Being a part of the construction crew would require getting dressed and leaving her house. She wasn't sure she was up for that. "I'm not sure."

"I will if you will," Melly said.

"I wish I could help," Gage said.

"Of course you can," Melly said. "We'll get you a special t-shirt that says 'Errand Boy' or something equally important." She ducked him when he reached for her, but either she didn't try too hard to get away or his reflexes were good because he caught her.

It was painful for Caleigh to watch them together, both because she hadn't decided yet if she was Team Gage or Team Kelsey and because there had never been that sort of rapport between her and Travis. She could see it now, could see how he had been trapped into marriage with her. Their dating relationship had been too brief and too casual to develop any sort of real bond. Their marriage had created a false sense of intimacy. Caleigh now realized it was much easier to share someone's bed than it was to share his heart. She knew every detail of Travis's body, but had no idea what was in his soul. And not for lack of trying. But he wouldn't open up, didn't want to open up because he didn't love her.

She might as well admit it: her marriage was a sham. Without the baby, there was no reason to stay. Before getting married, she judged people who divorced so easily. Now that she was facing a lifetime of loneliness and pain, she realized the decision to stay or go wasn't always so black and white. The more she thought about it, the more divorce seemed like the better option. She could start over with a clean slate, wiser this time. She was only nineteen. She could choose someone heart whole, someone who could love her in return.

Gage's eyes rested thoughtfully on her throughout the evening, but Caleigh didn't mind. He didn't seem to be judging her; he seemed to be trying to figure something out. Despite her reservations about leaving her house, the evening was nice. It was gentle and soothing, helped by the fact that she was never too far from Rocky. Either the dog had a sixth sense about who needed him, or he simply liked to have his ears rubbed because he hovered close to Caleigh like she was his new favorite possession. "I'll come back and visit," she whispered when Gage stood to take her home. Rocky's tongue rolled out and lapped at her face. She laughed as she wiped away his slobber.

Gage was quiet on the ride home. She thought maybe he was tired until he held her back before going inside. "Caleigh, I need to talk to you about something, but it's awkward. I don't usually involve myself in other people's marriages. But I do involve myself with Travis and…" he trailed off, disheveling his hair with his fingers. "The thing about Travis is that he would have you believe he changed after Mom's death. That's not true. The truth is that he was always difficult. Even when he was a baby he was a standoffish squealer. Mom and I were the only people he could really relate to. He and Dad never got along. Then Mom died, and it was like a part of him died, too. I'm the first person to admit he has issues. He's maddening. He can really drive you crazy. But underneath all that, he's a great kid with a great heart. Somewhere along the way he got mixed up, but I can't let go of this hope that he's going to get better, to find salvation again." His eyes fastened on her as if maybe she were the long-awaited salvation.

"I know I have no right to ask this after all you've been through but, please, don't give up on him so easily. Give him another chance. He has potential—I know it." He finished speaking but his eyes remained hopeful, pleading.

"I don't disagree with you Travis has potential," Caleigh said. "But do you know what happens to people who spend their days in a mine, looking for diamonds in the rough? They lose their lives to lung cancer. I want Travis to get better, I really do. But I'm not sure I have the stamina to see it through."

"I understand, and I'm not asking that of you. All I'm asking is for you to think about things before you do anything rash. Give it time. Don't do anything permanent while he's on deployment."

"I would wait to file until he comes back," Caleigh said.

Gage bit his lip at the finality of her words. "I brought some things, some of Travis's things." He reached behind him and lifted a large box from the back seat. "Our mom made scrapbooks for each of us to denote our childhoods. I thought maybe if you saw what Travis was like, if you got to know where he's been and who he was…" he trailed off, staring dejectedly at the box.

Caleigh rested her hand on his arm. "I'll look at them, of course I'll look at them."

He perked up and managed a smile. "I'll carry them inside for you."

She trailed behind him, curious. She had never seen pictures of Travis as a little boy. Gage set the box down and pulled her into a bone-crushing hug. "He loves you. I know it, even if he doesn't. Call me if you need me." He kissed her cheek, let her go, and let himself out. Caleigh waited until she heard him drive away, then she sat on the floor and began sorting through Travis's childhood.

CHAPTER 13

Kelsey stood and swore, the picture fluttering from his lap to the floor.

"What is it?" Travis snapped, annoyed he had been startled awake by the action.

"This picture Melly sent me. She's wearing a ring on her engagement finger. I swear if your brother proposed..." he let the sentence trail ominously away.

"Let me see," Travis commanded. Kelsey bent over and handed him the picture. He moved it in and out, adjusting it toward the light. There was a disembodied arm draped over Rocky, the dog. "You moron. That's not Melly's hand. That's Caleigh's hand, that's my ring." He stared at his wife's hand, a wave of longing and homesickness sweeping over him. Their comm satellite was spotty at best. With so many men wanting to speak to their loved ones, his talks with Caleigh had been few and far between.

"Let me see," Truck said, ripping the photo from Travis's fingers. "I think that's Shelby's hand."

Travis took it back, pointing. "No, look. Caleigh keeps her fingernails short so she can play guitar. And see those callouses on her fingers? That's from the guitar, too."

He looked up to see Kelsey and Truck grinning down at him. "Look who memorized his wife's hand," Truck said. "I think someone is in lurve."

Travis handed the picture back, embarrassed at having been caught in such a sentimental display of emotion. What was the big deal? So he knew what his wife's hand looked like. Didn't everybody? He turned his back to his teammates, staring blankly at the canvas wall of the tent, picturing Caleigh's hand as it lay on his chest. She slept curled toward him, her palm flat on his sternum. Sometimes when he woke, his hand was over hers, his fingers absently smoothing over the grooves left by her guitar. Why that memory above all the others should come to him now he didn't know. Their brief marriage had provided him with a movie reel of intimate scenes. Those were what should be playing in his head. Instead it was the little things—the way she smiled when the commercial with the little pig came on television, the way she closed her eyes and tipped her face up when they kissed.

Two months into deployment and I'm losing it, he thought. Not that he didn't have good reason. Everyone was having a rough time, not because conditions were stark—though they were—but because of the extreme boredom. There were thirty men in the wilderness doing absolutely nothing but laying sensors and trying not to get caught. They were men of action. When there was no action, what were they to do? Turn on each other, apparently. Everyone knew going in the assignment was going to be a soft op, but there was always the hope that "soft op" was the official word and there would be a few classified missions behind the lines. As it was, they had done nothing so far that couldn't be written on the front of any paper. In other words, they were bored out of their minds.

Tensions were high with all the men, but especially between Travis and Hanlan. They hadn't been at camp too many days before Hanlan came at Travis again, and this time Travis knew why—Hanlan had wanted his job. He had thought he was a shoe-in for the point man on the team until Travis was assigned. They had similar training, experience, and rank, but Hanlan firmly believed nepotism was to blame for

Travis's appointment. What bothered Travis the most was that he might be right. He had never mentioned his father, had never used his family connections to pave the way in his career. But doors had a way of opening for him in a fashion he found maddening. He had joined the marines as a manner of escaping his father. Why did the old man's reputation follow wherever he went? So his dad was an admiral. Big deal. That didn't mean Travis was a good soldier. He wanted his position based on his merits and not on his last name.

Knowing the reason for Hanlan's grudge helped Travis cope with the constant stream of insults. He was contrary enough to throw himself into the team to irritate his rival. *Eat your heart out, Hanlan. I'm point man and these are my best buds,* he thought as he ate with the team and spent his free time with them, too. The irony was that it was paying off in spades for his career. He actually was bonding with Truck and Kelsey. Everyone but Nick seemed to have fully accepted him as part of the team. And Nick's lack of response was due mostly to his new position. He wasn't their team leader anymore—he was their platoon leader, and he was busy. He walked a fine line between encouraging morale and quashing rebellion. The grumbling was said under everyone's breath, but people were starting to complain, to question, to talk. What were they doing there for so long if not to spy? They were right by the border, and yet as far as any of them knew they weren't to set foot in the other country. It was maddening.

Hanlan was a ringleader among the complainers. And even though Travis often thought the same things the other man said out loud, he feigned total allegiance to Nick to be in total opposition to Hanlan.

"Mail call," Private Cassidy yelled. Mail came from the base, a two hour drive each way. For that reason it only arrived twice a week. Letters from home were always a big deal, but with the addition of mind-numbing boredom they were on par with opening weekend of a blockbuster movie. Being married gave Travis entrée into a club he didn't realize existed until he was a part of it. There were four types of mail deliveries: mail from a girlfriend, mail from family, mail from strangers, and mail from a wife.

The mail from a girlfriend varied from high drama to high

romance. Letters were routinely stolen and read aloud and usually good for a laugh. Mail from family tended to be sincere yet boring. There were hand-drawn pictures from kids that inspired a few laughs, but in a lighthearted sort of way. Letters from parents were loaded with pleas to "be safe" and "come home in one piece." The tradeoff for such emotional baggage was usually in the form of food. Peanut butter, gum, beef jerky and candy could be found in many family packages. Deliveries from strangers such as schools or churches evoked a sort of deep patriotism and overall happiness. And then there were the letters from wives.

They weren't filled with as much gooey romance as the letters from the girlfriends. Sometimes there was some complaining and a little bit of resentment. But there was also a sort of intimacy and camaraderie, the type that only marriage can inspire. For one brief moment a soldier remembered there was someone at home who had his back, who cared about him with an unconditional sort of love that longed for his return if only to tell him off for being gone so long.

To Travis's dismay, Caleigh hadn't sent him any letters. Her family did, which was sort of heartening and annoying at the same time. They clearly didn't like or approve of him, but they were trying to be supportive. In each of these care packages was always a little note from Caleigh, but it was always odd, as if someone had bought a card, stuck it in front of her, and made her sign. He didn't understand it at all. So it was with no small amount of surprise that he found an actual letter waiting for him this time.

Dear Travis, he read. *I'm trying to remember everything wives aren't supposed to say when they write to their military husbands. I know "stay safe" is out, so I'll assume you're doing that anyway. Can I tell you I miss you? Because I do. Since I don't know exactly where you are, I can't really ask you what it's like there. I'll assume it's horrible and you miss home with real food and no MRE's.*

A few days ago, I spent the evening with Melly and Gage. It was fun, even though I was sort of a third wheel. Melly cooked and I always enjoy the chance to eat authentic Mexican food, even if my tongue was on fire for a few hours afterward. It occurred to me later that you've never eaten her cooking. You would love it, I think. I should also tell you I've fallen in love.

Here he stopped reading, gripping the paper so tightly his hand got a cramp. Whoever it was, he would kill him. Not in a euphemistic sense; he would literally kill him. Prison would be worth it. With effort, he forced himself to keep reading and find out with whom his wife was cheating.

He's the cutest, sweetest little thing. I say little, but he's huge. The name Rocky suits him somehow. Seriously, I love this dog. Maybe we should get one when you return. It helps wile away the lonely hours. I've become Melly's official dog sitter. Whenever she goes out for the evening, I'm dispatched to watch Rocky, and when she starts school she's going to drop him here for doggy-day camp.

Travis paused again, feeling like an idiot. Perhaps it was true when people said he too often acted without thinking. If he had gotten this letter at home, he would have ripped something up by now. As it was, he was forced to read on and realize he was jealous of a dog.

I've been doing a lot of thinking. About us. We have a lot to talk about when you get home. Things can't go on as they've been. I know I've made mistakes in our marriage, we both have. This is definitely not something we can discuss from a few thousand miles away. I guess I wanted you to know I'm thinking, really thinking, about our future. It would mean a lot to me if you would do the same. You said you didn't want me, and I know that's true. I see now how you were strong-armed into this marriage against your will. I guess I'm asking if you still want it. If you don't, when you return, you're free. I've woken up, so to speak, and I no longer want to be in a marriage with someone who doesn't want to be with me.

I'm pretty sure the above paragraph goes in the "what not to say to your military husband" pile. But I needed you to know I'm thinking about us, and I want to make sure you're thinking, too. Maybe this time apart is a good thing.

Wherever you are, I hope it's not too bad. Yours, Caleigh.

Travis sat back, stunned. What exactly was she saying? Was she saying she wanted a divorce? Where had that come from? What about the baby? The Caleigh he knew would rather die than be a single mother. There was something he was missing here, but he didn't know what. He reread the letter and still couldn't figure it out. He didn't think she was asking for a divorce, per se. Instead she seemed to be telling him he could have one if he wanted it. And she had signed the letter "Yours," not "Love." When had that happened? For months Caleigh had told him she loved him every day, even though he never reciprocated. When had that stopped? And why? Was it because she grew tired of being the only one to say it or was it because she stopped loving him?

Even though he hadn't been in love with her, he had liked knowing she loved him. It was a secure feeling to have her always there. Now that his freedom dangled before him, he didn't feel happy; he felt bereft. He had come to enjoy the new stability of his home life. What did he have to return to if he didn't have her? A nice truck and a cruddy apartment. No beautiful wife, no home-cooked food, no laundry services, no cleaning, no ordering of his finances. No Caleigh. Perhaps he was more emotionally immature than he realized because understanding that he would miss Caleigh's essence most of all was a big surprise. He would miss her sweetness, her softness, her gracefulness, her music. She was joy, light, and peace in a darkened world.

After his first few sentimental thoughts, he became angry. Who did she think she was to issue ultimatums to him? Their baby was half his. If she thought she could take off with it and cut him out of their lives, she had another think coming. He picked up a pen and paper to write a scathing response, but his hand froze. He stared at the blank paper, trying to frame a response. *Good riddance,* didn't feel right, but neither did, *Please don't leave me.* In the end, he said nothing. After all, she wasn't the one living in a wasteland, relying on letters to keep her sane. He didn't have to write to her. They could talk in person if the comm link ever went through. He would gage her frame of mind, and then maybe he would write a response. Caleigh was home, surrounded by her friends and family. She didn't need his support—she had it from all sides.

Convinced she didn't need to hear from him, he tucked her letter under his pillow and took his turn on duty.

* * *

A WEEK after her letter arrived in Travis's hands, Caleigh stood on a strange porch, most of her earthly possessions scattered at her feet. She knocked for a second time, holding her breath as she waited for the door to be answered.

At last it was. Caleigh and the Admiral stood on opposite sides of the door, sizing each other up. "You said if I ever needed anything, all I had to do was ask," Caleigh said.

"Yes," he agreed, his tone wary as he took in her bags.

"I need to get away from my well-meaning family for a while. They're driving me crazy."

He looked like he was choking on a gumball. "You want to stay here?"

"Is that okay?"

"Sure," he said, not sounding convinced at all. After a few more seconds of staring at her in stunned surprise, he opened the door, ushered her through, and picked up her bags in one fell swoop. He might be older, but the Admiral was apparently still in top physical condition. "I'll put you in the guest room," he said, leading the way.

"Actually, is it okay if I stay in Travis's old room?" she asked.

He froze again, turning to look at her with an expression that said, "I think you might be insane, but I'm willing to comply if it means keeping you subdued." "Sure," he said. Pivoting, he led the way down the opposite hall.

Travis's old room was exactly as he had left it. As Caleigh suspected, the Admiral either hadn't thought to redecorate or hadn't wanted to because of all the emotional turmoil such an action would cause. She had a sneaking suspicion about her father-in-law, but she wanted to get to know him a little better before she confirmed it.

"I don't want to interrupt your routine while I'm here," Caleigh said. "But I would love to help out and make myself useful. Do you have a cook?"

"I have a housekeeper. Sometimes she takes pity on my and leaves a few meals in the fridge for the week. Usually I eat in the mess hall at work." He was still staring at her as if she might be an apparition he had conjured from his own imagination. She almost expected him to reach out and pinch her to make sure she was real.

She beamed. "Great. I'll talk to her and see if I can take over cooking duties while I'm here."

"I work long, crazy hours," he warned.

"That's okay. I've had insomnia lately, so I'm on my own crazy schedule. We'll make it work."

"You don't have to cook. I'm happy to have you here as my guest."

"I like to earn my keep, but thank you. Hopefully I'll be gone before you're too sick of me."

He sighed. "You can stop pretending. I know you lost your rental house. How bad are things? Do you need some money?"

"We haven't lost our rental house. We have ten thousand dollars in our savings account. I really wanted to get away from my family and visit you."

His lashes fluttered. She had shocked him. She felt the unaccountable desire to giggle over that. His index finger scratched absently at his temple. "Well okay then. We'll make it work. Stay as long as you like." He backed out of the room, still keeping an eye on her as if not sure if she were friendly or a hostile.

She turned and surveyed Travis's room as she set her suitcase on the bed and started to unpack. Heavy metal posters decorated the walls, indicating a dark and disturbed teen. Caleigh had the idea that if she dug further, she would find some of the old anime and comic books his father had missed during the purge. The scrapbooks Gage gave her showed her a different side of the man she married. Instead of the cocky marine, she found a pudgy little boy with an eye patch who clearly didn't fit in—not at home, not a school, nowhere. There were a multitude of pictures of Travis, Gage, and their mom spending time together and having fun. Some of them were things Gage liked to do—all things athletic. But some of them were things Travis liked to do. Caleigh's favorite picture had been of the threesome at a comic book convention where they were all dressed like characters. Travis was beaming. Gage had looked chagrined, holding a light saber as if it were poison. But he had done it for the little brother he loved.

Whenever the Admiral was in a picture, it was always a Gage-themed activity—fishing, hunting, swimming, football. Travis hovered on the periphery of the photo looking miserable and left out. It was that expression that captivated Caleigh and sent her on her current mission because he wore that same expression all too often now—when he was with her family, when he was with his team. Was it possible all of his anger was a cover for feeling like an outsider? And, if so, how could she do what his mother had done? How could she love him for who he was?

At the very least the self-imposed assignment gave her a purpose, a reason to get up in the morning, a reason to set foot outside her house. Maybe she would find healing in Maryland with the Admiral, not only for herself, but for her husband, too.

Smiling now, she left the room and went to chat with her unsuspecting father-in-law.

The unrest was growing. Not that anyone would challenge Nick outright, or Kelsey, his second in command. Discipline and order were too engrained for that. But there were murmurs of unrest. Travis heard them, and he was torn.

On the one hand, he agreed. What were they here for if not to do recon? Night and day they walked the perimeter of the camp, staring down enemy territory that was within spitting distance, and yet they did nothing about it. Any work had long since run out. What next? That was what everyone wanted to know. They were done laying sensors for satellites. Why were they still there? The platoon was half hopeful they were about to send a squad behind the lines and half frustrated it hadn't happened already.

On the other hand, Travis had somehow become a part of the team, the inner core of men who were leading this mission. Nick was their commander, Kelsey their second, Truck their third and a squad leader. And then there was Travis. He wasn't officially anything, but being point man for the team endowed a certain amount of prestige. It must, or why else would people come to him with their problems and murmurs of discontent? Somehow he had become a go between for the grunts and command, a position he didn't want and was baffled to be in.

After much back and forth thought, he decided he owed more allegiance to Nick and his team than he did to the jumble of dissatisfied grunts, a realization that went against the grain. When had he started working for the man?

"You're quiet," Kelsey observed as he, Truck and Travis ate supper together. Nick never ate with them anymore. He seemed to be always doing something.

"Nothing wrong with being quiet," Truck interjected. "Some people believe that thinking before speaking is actually beneficial. Crazy, I know." They bickered a lot, but in a lighthearted, good natured way. Travis thought their leadership styles were indicative of their personalities. Kelsey was never quiet or still for long, but he was good at deflecting tension with humor or diversion. Truck was quieter and steadier, but all action when it came to solving problems. Nick factored somewhere in the middle. Quieter and steady like Truck but with charisma to match Kelsey's, he preferred to lead by inspiration. He was good at rallying morale with a few well-chosen words and a good example. He also seemed to take everything in stride, never freaking out or stressing about anything. Travis would never say so, but he appreciated how Nick was a strong leader without being domineering. He also thought the three worked well together. There was probably a reason they had been kept together so long. By this time they were like a well-oiled machine, anticipating each other before they could speak or act.

At times when he became philosophical and melancholy, like now, he couldn't help but compare himself to Lolly. They were doing it—he might as well join in. Lolly had been with the team a few years. No doubt his chemistry had been as strong as theirs. Beyond that he brought his own skill set to the table. His talent for black ops was legendary. Plus he had been a nice guy. Though short, his shadow was huge. Travis knew he would never measure up. What was the use of trying?

"Seriously, Dude, what is up? You look like someone stole your blankie," Kelsey said.

"Why haven't we gone in over there?" Travis asked. He nodded his head in the direction of the border.

"That's not why we're here," Kelsey said. Perhaps it was Travis's imagination, but he felt there was a lot being unsaid.

"I'm saying we're sitting right here, doing nothing, waiting for something. What? I can't help believe if we had someone with Lolly's skills, someone who could slip in and out undetected, we would have sent him by now and gotten on with whatever is going on here." He was playing a hunch, and it was working. Truck and Kelsey were darting each other looks. Either their poker faces stunk, or they were letting him in on the truth. "So why haven't we sent someone else?"

"We're working on it, okay?" Kelsey said. "The orders from up top are to only get in if we can get back out again. You know what it's like over there. At this stage in the game, we're not sure that's possible. We might have to call the mission a wash, but no one wants that, so we're giving it a little more time." His frustration was palpable. They hadn't been able to bring all the high-tech equipment that helped them get in and out undetected because the other side was watching, too. That would have been the equivalent of waving a red flag and shouting, "We're planning to sneak in and spy on you!" Instead they had brought only what was necessary for laying sensors and surviving, trying to make it seem as though that was what they were here for and nothing else. The sensor operation was a bluff, but only if they could figure a way to get in. The other country's paranoia knew no bounds. As they spoke, there was probably someone on the other side of the border having a meeting about how to make sure and keep the Americans out.

Travis presented the list of ideas he had been given by the rest of the platoon—all the ways everyone who wasn't in charge thought they could get in. Kelsey and Truck shot holes through them all. "We've thought of those and then some. There's no acceptable way to go about it yet. We're still thinking, though," Kelsey said. His dubious tone told Travis he doubted they would be able to think of a workable idea, which frustrated them all. They were the marines—they didn't do "no."

Resignedly, Travis took his leave. The meeting had left him feeling more frustrated and more caught in the middle. Before, he had identified with the rest of the platoon. His irritation was as high as theirs. What were they waiting for? Why did they sit on the border day after day doing nothing? Now he'd had a glimpse of the other side, and he saw things from their perspective. It wasn't as if they could simply stroll into a hostile country that was waiting and watching for them to make a move. They were at a standoff until they thought of some brilliant idea.

"Hey, Vega, heard from your wife lately?"

Travis considered pretending he hadn't heard Hanlan speak, but ignoring things wasn't really in his nature. "What's it to you, Hanlan?" Some weariness crept into his tone. He was tired of dealing with Hanlan and his barbs. Hanlan had at first tried picking fights over the Admiral, but Travis was impervious to that. He had heard the taunts about special treatment and nepotism for years. That was why it didn't work when Hanlan tried to use Nick as a lever, either, especially because that one was unequivocally untrue. Travis received no special treatment for being the commander's brother-in-law. Having decided for himself his barbs weren't landing where he wanted, Hanlan moved on to the one thing guaranteed to get a rise—Travis's wife.

So far Travis had kept his cool, but he was quickly losing patience. He didn't like hearing Caleigh's name on Hanlan's lips, or seeing the creepy leer on his face whenever they happened to meet. A good girl like Caleigh wouldn't be safe crossing paths in a dark alley with a guy like Hanlan.

Hanlan shrugged, the expression Travis hated smeared all over his features. "Someone's gotta be there to pick up the pieces when you and the little Mrs. crash and burn. Might as well be me."

What do you know, I do have a boiling point, Travis thought as he took a swing. Hanlan gave one, gleeful smile before diving in with both fists, and then it was over all too soon.

"Hanlan, were you trying to steal Vega's lunch money again?" Kelsey asked. He held the two men as far from each other as his long arms would allow. There was something to be said for having a height advantage.

"Let me go so I can send him home in a box," Travis said. His anger was gone, replaced by cool determination. It was time to end things with Hanlan once and for all.

"I'm not going to let you kill him out here in the middle of nowhere," Kelsey said. "We're going to do it in front of the rest of the platoon so we can be amused and take bets on the outcome. Meet back here at nineteen hundred hours, bare knuckles, no weapons." He released them. Hanlan shrugged away and walked off, but Travis remained.

"Why are you doing this?" he asked. Fights, even those half-heartedly sanctioned by command, could get them in a lot of trouble—Kelsey most of all because he was putting his seal of approval on things.

"Because the men need some entertainment, because this has been building since the beginning and we might as well get it over with, and because I want you to crush him so he'll shut up. He's getting on my nerves."

"All right," Travis said. Kelsey watched him walk away and thought either Travis was growing as a person or he was growing on him. When they first met, Kelsey was sure Travis was full of hot air and bluster, that he was an unreliable loose cannon. He might still be a messed up kid, but there was something there, something deeper. The cockiness wasn't hot air, it was him saying whatever he believed and whatever came to mind. He might be a jerk, but he was a genuine jerk, and Kelsey sort of appreciated that about him. He didn't pretend to be a great guy with high moral standards. He was what he said he was—a messed up marine trying to do his best. He liked to party, but he was young. When it came to work, he was all business, and he did it without complaint. In time, Travis had the potential to be a good guy and an excellent marine.

Nick came up beside him and scanned the horizon. "Should I be concerned my second in command is staring into space with a dreamy expression?"

"Probably," Kelsey said. "But you should be even more concerned I sanctioned a fight between two of the men. It might be best to make yourself scarce at nineteen hundred, Lieutenant. What you don't know can't hurt you."

Nick blinked at him and scratched his temple. "I'm beginning to lose track of all the conversations I'm not supposed to be having with you."

Kelsey grinned. "This one is definitely at the top of the list. I'll let you know how the fight turns out."

In answer, Nick sighed and turned away, shaking his head.

* * *

WHEN THE GROUP of marines assembled to watch the fight, there was so much bloodlust in the air Travis felt like a gladiator of old. Or maybe he was a slave sent to meet his doom. The odds were split fairly evenly between him and Hanlan, so it could go either way, at least according to the crowd who had hedged their bets down the middle. According to Travis, there could only be one outcome: total annihilation.

For two marines who were well-matched in size, strength and training, hand-to-hand combat could last a long time. Travis stood on the sidelines before the fight, chowing down on a protein bar and guzzling some water to prepare. He hoped he didn't break any teeth this time. Injuries in the field were commonplace and, at least for Travis, so were fist fights. Of all the injuries he had sustained, broken teeth hurt the worst. The medics kept dental wax on hand to seal any holes, but that was the best they could do for the next few months. There were no dentists in the field, unfortunately.

Kelsey called the fight and laid out the rules or, rather, the rule: "Don't kill each other." Travis and Hanlan began circling each other in the ancient dance of two men about to fight, sizing each other up, looking for weakness. There was a time when Travis was new and had more to prove that he would have made the first move. Age and experience had provided wisdom. Fights were often like a game of college football—a good defense could mean the difference between winning and losing. So he waited Hanlan out, offering up his most obnoxious expression in the hopes of provoking an attack. He didn't have to wait long.

Hanlan swung at his face, trying to knock the smugness away, and Travis used the opening to jab his ribs, hard. Hanlan made a satisfying "oof" sound as the air whooshed from his lungs. In a street fight with a civilian, it probably would have been enough to topple him, but marines were more resilient and Hanlan looked no worse for having had the wind knocked out of him. They circled each other for a while longer before Hanlan took another swing. Travis was delighted to learn he was fighting angry, as if he had taken all the resentment he bore toward Travis and bottled it to give himself energy.

Travis laughed because as much as he hated Hanlan, he wasn't fighting angry. To fight angry was to lose. Winning required a clear, cool head. His laughter annoyed Hanlan even more so that he dove at him, butting his head into Travis's stomach in a maneuver that knocked them both to the ground. They rolled round and round, unable to land a blow, scrabbling with their knees and feet as they scuffled in the dirt.

In a real situation, such an encounter was often cause for panic because it was like the death throes of any confrontation. Similar to watching a crocodile thrash an unsuspecting wildebeest in the water, writhing for supremacy in a fight was no less daunting or exhausting. The mind tended to go to its most primal survival mode. *Think,* Travis commanded. This was where battles were won or lost. When men stopped thinking and started reacting, they lost. When they kept their wits and strategized, they won.

Step one was to get off the ground. He broke free from Hanlan's entangling grasp around his neck, jabbed him in the stomach with his knee, and used it as a springboard to stand up. Hanlan wasn't far behind. Travis whirled to see his opponent standing and charging again. He sidestepped him and sent Hanlan sprawling to the dirt face first. He came up spitting.

The fight went on and on. Since Travis knew he wanted to be in Special Forces, he had trained hard in hand-to-hand combat. He had spent hours wrestling other marines in torrential downpours, wearing full gear, after being fogged with pepper spray. Special Forces had also been Hanlan's aim, though. He had probably spent an equal amount of time in the same kind of training. Neither of them would go down easily, neither would give up without a fight to the finish.

The fight must have been getting good from a spectator's point of view because the mood of the crowd shifted from enthusiasm to tension. He could hear them grunting as blows were delivered and taken, as if they were the ones duking it out. Some of them probably wished they were. Inactivity was a killer, boredom their arch nemesis. Travis was beginning to think he might appreciate a little boredom again. His eye was starting to swell, his mouth filling with blood. Still, he didn't stop. Instead he spat it out and kept fighting.

When it began to look as if the fight could go on all night, Travis received one of those lucky breaks that sometimes but rarely happens —Hanlan messed up. He faked too far left in an attempt to land a kidney punch. Travis used the momentum to grab his arm, spin him, and take him down. With one satisfying tug and snap, his shoulder was out of its socket. To his credit, he didn't scream. Travis comforted himself with the knowledge that it would hurt as much when the medics popped it back in.

"Done?" Travis asked, still wrenching the now-useless arm behind his opponent's back.

"Done," Hanlan agreed.

Travis backed away warily. He didn't trust Hanlan's word. Just because he was down didn't mean he was out. It would be like him to attack while Travis was retreating. And he did, but not physically.

"Good fight, man," he said, slinging his dangling appendage to the front as if it were detached from his body. "No hard feelings. And, hey, I'm really sorry about the baby."

It took a lot to silence a crowd of rowdy marines, but that was what happened. The thirty or so men in attendance all went deathly still, all except Kelsey who stepped forward and hauled Hanlan to his feet. "Shut up and get to a medic before I slam what's left of your teeth down your throat."

"What was he talking about?" Travis asked. He was sweating rivulets all over his body, but he was cold, the kind of cold that comes from dread.

The answering quiet was deafening. Kelsey took another step forward, gesticulating wildly. "He…You know Hanlan is…The thing is…"

Travis's dread grew. Whatever it was, it must be bad if Kelsey was at a loss for words. Truck stepped forward and faced the assembled crowd. "Break it up." They dispersed as if by magic, without protest, without laughter, just quietly shuffled away. Truck watched them go and turned back to Travis. "Caleigh lost the baby. I'm sorry."

Kelsey winced. "Geez, Ashton. Sensitive much?"

"He deserved to know from the beginning. There was no easy way to say it," Truck replied.

"What do you mean she lost the baby? She was five months along when we left," Travis said. His mind refused to accept the information.

"I guess when they're that far along it's not a miscarriage anymore. It's a stillbirth. She had the baby; he didn't make it."

"He?" Travis said. *Tucker,* he thought, remembering Caleigh's name for a boy. "When did this happen?"

"The day we deployed," Kelsey said. He sounded miserable. Good. He should feel miserable.

Travis remembered the way everyone went silent when Hanlan said the words. "Did everyone know but me?"

"Caleigh didn't want you to know," Kelsey said. "She didn't want you to worry."

"Did everyone know but me?" Travis asked again.

Truck nodded. "We didn't say anything to anyone. But the women have been working together on Ashleigh's kitchen. They talked, and they told their husbands."

There was only one way an entire platoon had kept something so monumental from one man. "Did Nick give the order not to tell me?" Travis asked.

"We were waiting until it was closer to the end of the mission. It's a helpless feeling to be so far away when you're wife is going through something," Kelsey said.

"How would you know?" Travis snapped. "You don't have a wife." He turned his back on them, trying to compose his broiling emotions. "I need to talk to Nick."

"Why don't you take a breath and calm down first?" Truck suggested.

"Why don't you stop telling me what to do?" Travis yelled, whirling to face them again. In that moment, he wanted to kill them, to kill all of them. His emotions were too hot to put a name to, but one thing was certain: he *needed* to see his brother-in-law, the sooner, the better. "I'm not a child, I'm not your kid brother, I'm not Lolly. I don't need your protection or your compassion. Now tell me where he is."

"He's in the mess hall," Truck said. Resignation and regret were heavy in his tone. Later it would go a long way with Travis that Truck had wanted to tell him, that he hadn't agreed with Caleigh's decision to keep him out of the loop. Not right now, though. Right now he was out for blood.

Truck and Kelsey followed behind him, dogging his heels like two delinquent bodyguards, ready to rein him in if he lost it and went postal on their precious commander. He pushed out his palm and slammed through the flap of the tent, shoving it roughly out of his way. Nick's head jerked up in question that quickly changed to understanding as soon as he saw a bruised and bloody Travis being flanked by Truck and Kelsey. He sat back with a look Travis had seen on the Admiral's face many times, as if he knew the fight was coming and was ready to defend his position.

"I want to go on the mission," Travis blurted, taking everyone by surprise.

"What?" Nick said.

"I want to go. I want to be the one sent over."

"No," Nick said.

"Yes," Travis argued.

"No," Nick repeated.

"Yes, and I'll tell you why. I've been trying to convince everyone here I'm not getting special treatment because I'm your brother-in-law, and then I learn I've been lying all along. I have been getting special treatment."

"You haven't," Nick argued.

"Tell me you would have kept a dead baby from any other man in this unit because his wife asked you to, and I'll believe you," Travis said.

Nick's lips pressed together in a grim line. "When you put it that way, I see your point. But that doesn't mean I'm willing to send you into a country you have no chance of returning from. And I don't need one man. I need a team."

"You need a team and a distraction," Travis said. "I'm your distraction."

Nick was going to say no again, Travis could feel it. "If it were Lolly, would you say yes?" Travis asked.

Nick deflated. "Probably. But Lolly was gifted more than any other man I know, myself included."

"I'm point man for this team, and I didn't get that position with my good looks. I have my own set of skills, and it's time you let me use them. If I'm going to get special treatment, then I want it to be for something I want. And I want this. I want to go."

This was the one of the hardest decisions Nick had been forced to make. If Travis went and became injured or killed on his orders, Caleigh would never forgive him. Then again, Travis had a point: it wasn't really about his sister-in-law. He needed to differentiate between the job and his family. If Travis wasn't married to his beloved little sister, what would Nick do?

"All right, you can go," Nick said. "Kelsey's heading up the recon team. Any suggestions for a point man to replace you?"

"Hanlan," Travis said. "I hate the guy, but he can take a beating. I've been watching him and, while I think he's a terrible excuse for a man, he's a good soldier, a good point man."

"Hanlan it is," Nick said.

"You're going to have to wait until he's out of the sick bay," Kelsey said with a little too much satisfaction. He and Truck snickered. Travis didn't join in. If they thought his anger and raw, disjointed emotions had burned themselves out, they were mistaken. He bumped by them and went back to his bunk, grabbed his stuff and took what passed for a shower by their primitive standards. Basically it was little more than a hose filtered through a bucket with holes, but Travis didn't care. The cold water stung his many scrapes, but the pain felt good because it was a distraction from thinking about what was going on inside him. Caleigh hadn't wanted him to know their baby died. Fine. He wouldn't think about it. From now on, life would be one big distraction until he arrived home. After that, it was anybody's guess about what would happen next.

CHAPTER 15

"Smells good in here."

Caleigh finished setting the table as soon as her father-in-law walked through the door. "Thank you," she said. He washed his hands and sat as the last dish landed on the dining room table. In Caleigh's world, her family ate at the kitchen table. The dining room was reserved for special occasions and visitors. In the Admiral's world, only breakfast was eaten in the kitchen. Supper was in the formal dining room, even when he ate alone. Instead of feeling stifled by the formality, Caleigh found it quaint. She had come to the man expecting to meet the devil, and instead found a friend. Caldwell Vega might run a tight ship, so to speak, but he was a pushover when it came to his daughter-in-law. The more Caleigh got to know him, the more she was of the opinion that what existed between Travis and his father was a colossal misunderstanding and lack of communication.

"How was your day?" Caleigh asked.

"No one died," the Admiral said, the same answer he had every day. She supposed he was half joking and half serious since people probably did occasionally die on his watch. "What did you do today?"

"I spent some time at the VA." In an odd sort of way, Caleigh was making a life for herself here, more than she had made while living at home. After introducing her to his friends and associates, the Admiral left her alone, giving her time to think, to reflect, to breathe. She had been surrounded by people who offered their overwhelming love and support her whole life, and she wasn't complaining. She knew how blessed she was, knew their careful love and attention had made her the person she was. The problem was that she didn't know who that was. Who was Caleigh Desmond Vega without her husband and family? For the first time in her life, she was finding out.

"Do-gooder," Caldwell accused. He was one to talk—he spent an inordinate amount of time with injured vets and their families. He might occasionally be prickly to deal with, but his moral compass was as sure as hers.

"What was your wife like?" Caleigh asked. After working up her courage for the past couple of weeks, she finally blurted the question that had been weighing on her mind.

Caldwell choked. A less polite man would have sputtered. Instead, he dabbed his napkin against his lips. "I didn't see that question coming."

"You don't have to talk about her if you don't want," Caleigh said.

"You took me by surprise, but I'm happy to talk about her. Margaret was a saint, first and foremost. She put up with me and the boys." His eyebrows drew together. "Well, not Gage so much. I swear that kid was born with good manners and a head full of self-discipline. But Travis put her through the paces, not that she would ever let on how much he exhausted her. She was always trying to keep him busy, keep him entertained, keep him engaged."

"Keep him engaged?" Caleigh repeated.

"He had a tendency to disappear into his own little world. Gage and I could toss a ball and talk about stuff. Travis would stand there, staring. You'd throw a ball at him, and it would bounce off his noggin. That should have been a sign of how hard his head was."

"And yet he turned into an incredibly athletic marine," Caleigh pointed out.

"Maybe it was all those laps I made him run for talking back," the

Admiral said, something between chagrin and fondness in his smile. "Never seen a kid hate running more."

"You love him," Caleigh blurted.

The Admiral shifted as he reached for more potatoes. "Everyone loves their children, Caleigh."

She didn't think he simply loved Travis because he had to. Not wanting to press the matter, she urged him to keep talking. "You were telling me about your wife."

"Oh, right, Margaret. She was born to be a military wife. The woman never complained, not when we moved every year or two, not when I was deployed for two year stretches—never. If there was trouble at home, I never heard about it. She sent me off with a smile and greeted me the same way." He paused, sighing. "Makes me feel even guiltier about all the hell I put her through."

"How so?" Caleigh asked.

"I wasn't always the model of strength and discipline you see before you." His eyes twinkled, letting her know he was being self-deprecating. "My early life was chaotic and abusive. I probably would have followed that same path if not for Margaret and the navy. One taught me discipline and the other gave me an unbreakable inner strength. I'll leave it to you to figure out which was which. Suffice it to say Margaret showed me a home could be a loving, secure place to come back to. In the beginning, I viewed us as combatants. After a while, I realized we were teammates. The last few years were blissful, even if she was sick. Thanks to her, I finally understood what it meant to love and be loved in return. That's a rare gift, to be loved and know it."

She was sure he hadn't meant to make her cry, but the effect was the same. Her eyes welled. She dropped her fork to swipe at them. "Travis doesn't love me," she said.

"How could he not?" the Admiral said. "You're lovely, so much like my Margaret—the kind of person who makes the world better by being in it."

Caleigh shook her head. "I wish...but he doesn't. I'm afraid of what's going to happen when he comes home. I'm afraid that without the baby, he'll want out."

"If that's the case, then he's even more of a fool than I think he is," the Admiral said.

"He's not a fool," Caleigh said, her tone vehement. "He's exactly like you. Can't you see that?"

Caldwell blinked at her, probably wondering if she had taken leave of her senses. "No, I don't see that at all." He sounded so confused that Caleigh laughed as she swiped at her eyes again.

"I see it. You and Gage may have had some common interests, but you're nothing alike. Travis is a rounder, like his dad. I married the second most hard-headed, stubborn man to ever walk the planet, his father being the first. Once he sets his mind to something, there's no changing it; there's no changing *him.* I'm the first to admit he has faults, but all the basic elements of goodness are there. He simply has to learn to tap into them the way you did."

His finger inched up to scratch his temple. "You think Travis and I are alike," he drawled.

Caleigh nodded. "He wanted to make his own way by joining the marines. Really, is that anything different than what you would have done if it was what you wanted?"

One side of his mouth quirked into a smile. "My old man didn't want me to be a diver. Said it would divert me from my career. I did it anyway, of course. He also didn't want me to marry Margaret. He thought I couldn't handle being a family man and career navy."

"Sounds like there are a lot of apples falling close to their trees in this family," Caleigh noted.

"You think the reason Travis and I have so much trouble getting along isn't because we have nothing in common, but rather because we're so much alike." He said it apprehensively, like someone trying to puzzle together the pieces of a mystery.

"Yes, I think so," she said. "I see two strong men, both unbending when they think they're right. And both of you think you're right most of the time."

"All of the time, really." He chuckled. "I'll let you be the one to tell him this piece of information. He won't hit you." He paused, scowling. "Will he? He doesn't hit you, does he?"

"Of course not," Caleigh said, affronted all over again.

Caldwell nodded. "I didn't think so, but sometimes people are good at hiding things like that. My father, for instance. No one would ever guess that such a respected navy man beat his wife and children. I may have had my issues with Travis, but I never touched my boys or their mother." He blew out a breath. "I guess I messed up in other ways, though. What else am I to believe when one of my sons hates me so much?"

"He doesn't hate you," Caleigh said.

He quirked an eyebrow at her.

"He's angry at you," Caleigh conceded.

"I did what I thought was best. How could it have been good for him to spend all his time in his room playing with those lifeless video games? When Gage was home, at least he had a friend. But after Gage left for school, I had to step in and make sure Travis was okay, to make sure he grew into the kind of man I knew he could be. I couldn't stand to see him burying his face in some comic book instead of talking to people, instead of really living. Maybe I pushed him a little too hard, but it was for his own good. When he has kids, he'll understand that."

Caleigh blanched, and the Admiral noticed. "I'm sorry, Caleigh. That was an insensitive thing to say."

"It's okay," she said. He hadn't meant to bring up the baby. She had never realized before how much people talked about babies and children in everyday conversation. Now she was sensitized to every mention, but it wasn't the fault of the speaker. No one was purposely trying to rub salt into her wounds.

They ate in silence a few minutes, each one lost in thought. Caleigh was thinking about her perfect little son whose only defect had been his too-early arrival. The hospital had let her hold him as long as she wanted, but it wasn't long enough. How could something so perfect be gone?

The Admiral was thinking about Travis and Margaret and how

things would have been different if she had lived. She would have been a buffer between them as they tried to navigate the difficult adolescent years. She wouldn't have let so much space and animosity come between them. She would have shown them how to talk to each other, how to relate. His phone rang, and he pulled it from his pocket to check the number.

"Excuse me, Caleigh, this is work. They only call for emergencies." He answered the phone and sat back. Caleigh watched as the color drained from his face. His eyes flicked to her and quickly away again. "Yes, I see. Thank you, sir. Yes, thank you."

Who did the Admiral call sir? There were only a handful of people higher on the chain of command than he was. Why would any of them be calling in the middle of supper? Caleigh was curious, but she had learned not to ask nosy questions when it came to the military. Practically everything was classified, a need-to-know reality that a wife apparently didn't need to know. Sometimes she wondered if things were really so secret or if it was one more way of strengthening the bond that made military men feel like they were set apart. *The fleet is out of toilet paper, sir. Let's keep this classified.*

"I need to go out of town for a while, Caleigh," Caldwell said and, just like that, he was gone. He didn't even have to pack. He simply walked up the stairs, grabbed a bag of clothes and toiletries he always kept at the ready, and walked back out, all while Caleigh sat at the table and stared. Then she started to worry. What sort of an emergency would claim a four-star admiral from the supper table? Were they at war? Was a nuclear bomb heading toward the country at this very moment? Possibilities ran through her head, possibilities fueled by Hollywood and years of watching television and movies. But never in her wildest thoughts did she imagine the emergency in question was the disappearance of her very own husband.

CHAPTER 16

Travis had a lot of time to review the situation and wonder if the outcome could have been different. He kept coming back to the resounding answer that he had done what he needed to do. He was the decoy. He hadn't *wanted* to get caught, but it was always a possibility. The possibility had turned into a necessity when an enemy squad had almost stumbled on the team. *Now's the time, decoy,* he had told himself before he stood and walked into the clearing. He had fully expected to be shot. He should have known life never works as planned. Instead of shooting him on sight, they had taken him prisoner. In the world of guerilla warfare, an American soldier was the gold standard of currency. They would undoubtedly kill him, but not before they tried to get as much out of him as possible.

In a weird way, the fight with Hanlan had helped to stave off the inevitable beatings and torture. What was the fun of beating someone who already looked like his face had been run through a meat grinder? Instead they threw him in a cage with a few exclamations of disgust at not being the ones who got to him first. Or so Travis imagined. In reality, he didn't speak the language and had no idea what they were saying. All he knew was that his life had become a waiting game. He could almost feel the seconds ticking away, leaving him with nothing to do but think. And since he refused to think about the future and what was coming for him, that left him only the past. He started with the immediate past, reviewing the operation to see if there was anything he could have done differently. No, he had done what he needed to do. His captors had been so focused on him he was sure the team had been able to get in and back out again without being caught.

Next his mind moved to the topic that was almost as painful as the coming torture. Caleigh had lost the baby, and she hadn't told him. How could she have kept something like that from him? *I didn't want you and I didn't want the baby.* His own words echoed back to him. She didn't think he meant that, did she? He had told her he didn't mean it. Hadn't he? Had he ever told her how much she had come to mean to him? How excited he was about becoming a father? No, because he hadn't known what to say and because he hadn't wanted to give her that kind of power over him. Now he was going to die in some enemy camp without ever having told his wife he loved her. What kind of man took all Caleigh had given without giving anything in return?

"I should be shot," he muttered, then laughed when he realized he probably would be. The man who was standing watch as his guard scowled at his laughter and kicked the cage. "Those are some tiny feet, man," Travis said. "I didn't know they made combat boots that small." The guard had no idea what he was saying, but he didn't seem to care for Travis's tone. He jabbed at his head with the butt of his rifle until Travis made a grab for it. He realized his mistake in time to take a few steps back and yank the rifle out of reach. Furious now, he turned the rifle around and pointed it at Travis's midsection. "You're going to shoot me because you're stupid? Go ahead, but your buddies aren't going to be happy when they realize you killed their new toy."

Either he did understand a little bit of English, or he was thinking it through for himself because he lowered the gun and said a whole bunch of what sounded like angry gibberish to Travis.

"So's your mother," Travis said, and the guard kicked the cage again.

Travis laughed again. So much of being a marine was a mind game, and this was where Travis had the advantage over most other soldiers. He had been playing war with the Admiral for most of his life, bottling up his feelings and putting up a false front. By now he was a pro. "You think you can get to me?" he taunted. "My dad burned my mint anime collection. Now *that* was torture." The guard was trying to ignore him now, but that was fine with Travis. It left him more time to think, to make one last review of his life before the pain became too intense for introspection. The marines, in all their wisdom and kindness, had prepared their men to be captured and tortured. Travis knew exactly what his mind and body were in for. It was best not to think about it, better to think of all the things he wouldn't live to see again. What would he miss the most?

He settled back against the bars of the cage as much as he could, ignoring the cramping that was already taking over his legs that could neither bend nor straighten. "I Lance Corporal Travis Vega, being of somewhat sound mound and mostly sound body, do hereby bequeath…" He stopped. What did he have to bequeath? His truck? He had a few thousand dollars in the bank, but that was thanks to Caleigh. What did he have to give that was really his? The answer didn't come. Instead he started to sing an off-key rendition of the star spangled banner, not stopping until the end, even when his captor started beating on his cage.

* * *

Even in the midst of a crisis, everyone knew the moment Admiral Caldwell Vega's helicopter touched down. The military had its own version of superstar awe—usually inspired by the rare glimpses of someone as high up the chain of command as the Admiral. This sighting was no exception. Men stopped what they were doing and stared as he stepped from the chopper and headed toward the camp's makeshift command. It wasn't only imagination that set him apart; he was impeccably clean while most of them had gone too long without a shower. He walked with purpose, his hat tucked under his arm so it wouldn't blow away. Then he disappeared into the tent and life resumed its normal pace. The show was over, at least for the men standing watch. For the men inside the tent, the show had only begun.

"I want to know what's being done," he said. His eyes scanned the interior of the tent until they rested on Nick with dislike and suspicion. The feeling inside the tent was less awed and more frustrated. What everyone agreed they didn't need right now was Washington brass breathing down their necks, father of their missing soldier or not.

Since they were indoors with their hats off, there was no need to salute, but they couldn't help but come to attention. "Good afternoon, Sir," Nick said, coming over with his hand extended. The Admiral shook it more out of habit than courtesy. Nick knew he would have received an update on the situation and their mission, even though it was under the highest security clearance. Apparently someone higher up felt that family ties trumped security. The breach irritated Nick in ways he didn't understand. If it were his son who had been captured, he would want to know. On the other hand, shouldn't the rules be the same for everyone? "Our mission was a success in terms of information retrieval. Unfortunately it didn't contain information about the location of their base. Today's satellite images have provided us with a few possibilities, but they seem to have set up bluffs. Right now we're working on determining which is their actual camp." It went without saying they would have one shot at a rescue. After that, Travis would be moved again. The country in question was so good at keeping secrets they might never find him.

"You're sure he's still in the area?" the Admiral said.

"There have been no choppers or transports in or out. Unless they're on foot, they're still here. And none of us sees them hiking that far with a prisoner who could kill them at the first hint of freedom." Assuming Travis wasn't already dead or injured beyond his ability to function, he would be a danger to them. If he was lucky, they would underestimate him and leave an unguarded moment for him to escape. If they were smart, they would take every precaution and not give him the opportunity to inflict any damage. Marines were not trained to be docile prisoners. Marines were trained to fight back.

"Let me see the Sat images."

"Right this way, sir," Nick said. He stepped aside and let the Admiral lead them to the table where a half dozen images were spread. They were nearly identical with mounds that resembled bunkers, and dots that denoted men as guards. The Admiral squinted as though trying to see something the other half dozen men in the room hadn't. Which one of these locales held his son? "Logic tells us this is the one," Nick said, pointing to the picture on the far right. "It's closest to the river and near the edge of this trail that could be a supply line."

The Admiral caught something in the younger man's tone. "But you don't think this is the one," he said, tapping the photo.

"No, sir, I don't. My gut tells me it's too obvious. If there's anything we've learned about the other side since we've been here, it's that their paranoia knows no end. They wouldn't settle in the most likely place. I think this is the one." He tapped the picture in the middle. "It's the least likely place, surrounded by dense vegetation, far from water, and practically invisible except for the expertise of our satellites. If we weren't looking, we would never find it. But because they know we're looking, they've set up the other bluffs to confuse us."

"What's being done to find out for sure?" the Admiral asked.

"Nothing," Nick said. "There's nothing we can do but make a guess and aim for the best."

"That's not good enough, Lieutenant," the Admiral said.

Nick scanned the room of people listening with baited breath. "Could you leave us alone, gentlemen?" He waited to speak again until they were alone. "I realize, sir, this is your son. But it's for that reason you're too close to the situation. You need to give me space to do my job."

"I'm not leaving this to chance, not leaving it to a lieutenant on his first command."

"With all due respect, sir, you don't know these men, you don't know this terrain, and your presence here is a courtesy."

"Son, I have been dealing with situations like this since you were in diapers. I know what I'm doing."

"If I have questions, I will certainly ask, but I happen to know what I'm doing, too. You can't see how emotionally involved you are here, but I do. You've lost your objectivity. The best thing you can do for Travis right now is to stand back, get out of my way, and let me retrieve my point man."

Caldwell's fist clenched and relaxed a few times. He hadn't gotten into a fistfight with anyone since he was in the academy, but he was tempted to do so now. Perhaps the young lieutenant had a point after all. "I think I should tell you that if you mess this up then your career has reached its end," he said, controlling his tightly coiled rage with effort.

"I think I should tell you that when the life of one of my men is at stake, I couldn't care less about my career. Now if you'll excuse me, sir, I have work to do." With a nod of dismissal, Nick turned his back to the man and began studying the satellite images again.

With nothing to do and no one to command, Caldwell was at a loss. Slowly, the other men began to stream back into the control center. The Admiral eased into a chair and sat down, watching someone else lead for the first time in his thirty year career.

CHAPTER 17

Travis had lost his sense of humor, but he wasn't broken. His fingers were, all ten of them, but his spirit was still intact. His fingernails had been pulled from their beds, a few of his ribs were cracked, but otherwise he was in good shape, especially considering what more could have been done to him. Not that they were finished with him. They were simply letting him rest, letting him think about what they might be plotting next. He didn't have to think, though; he knew. He saw the battery, the cables, the water. A few broken fingers were about to feel like a paper cut in comparison.

There was a certain amount of dread in his heart, but no fear. They were far from done with him and not ready to kill him yet. Back home, he had elected to be water boarded so he would know what it felt like. He had also been shocked once to get a taste of the torture. Ten seconds of being drowned and a mild electrical impulse had convinced him he never wanted to feel either again, and they were nothing in comparison to what was coming. But that was the point of preparation—to prepare. He wasn't excited about the prospect, but he wasn't afraid. He would live, and that was what mattered now. Survival mode for a soldier didn't necessarily involve remaining intact, it simply meant remaining alive. He might be irreparably broken, but he would still be living. In the end, that was all that was important.

For a while as they ripped out his nails, he had found solace by imagining a rescue operation. His friends would arrive and wreak havoc. That thought had been so satisfying he had managed a laugh. The laugh so enraged his captors that they used a board to bash him in the chest, cracking several ribs. After that everything went a little hazy until he landed back in his cage. Now his mind was clearing again and he could hear boot steps scrabbling in the dirt. They were coming for him. Quickly his mind scrambled for something to protect itself. They could have his body, but they would never take his mind. The only way to ensure that, though, was to focus on something else. But what? What was powerful enough to hold his focus while he was going through what he was getting ready to go through?

He conjured the image of his teammates, but that quickly dissipated. The longer time passed, the less likely they were to find him alive. His captors arrived at his cage and unlocked it. Travis thought of Gage. His brother's ghost walked beside him a few paces, offering up encouragement. "You can do this, Pal," the pretend Gage whispered. "Think of it like a trip to the dentist, if the dentist was trying to drown and electrocute you. You've got this. I'm right here. I won't leave." But he did leave. As soon as the guards pushed open the door to their torture chamber, Gage disappeared, leaving Travis unbearably alone.

His father arrived next, stern and unsmiling as he took in the scene. Travis wished he was real. The old man might be a pain sometimes, but he was tough, tough enough to tear the place apart with his bare hands. Despite their differences, Travis had no doubt that if his father was present, there would be a pile of dead bodies on the floor. That thought almost made him smile. He didn't often think of his father as a soldier. He would like to see him in action someday, to see him use his power for good instead of evil.

Two men pushed him into a chair and tightened the straps. Travis didn't struggle. He was too weak and outnumbered to be effective.

Instead he decided to use his energy where he most needed it —mentally.

"Why are you here?" The question was asked in English so heavily accented Travis thought the speaker didn't know what he was saying. He had probably translated the question on the internet and practiced it until he could say the words correctly. He imagined the man standing in front of a mirror, holding his card and repeating his phrase over and over, trying to sound scary and literate.

"Just take a little off the top. You took too much last time, and my head looked lopsided," Travis said. The man stared at him, clearly having no idea what he was saying. But it didn't matter. They didn't actually want information, they wanted retaliation—retaliation for Travis's invasion into their country as well as for centuries of poverty and unfairness. Someone needed to pay for their pain, and with an American soldier in their midst, they had the perfect vehicle for retribution. So it wouldn't matter if Travis remained silent or if he spilled every secret he had ever known; the outcome was already predetermined.

He took a breath before they shoved his head under the water, but it didn't make a difference. He still felt like he was drowning. Probably because he was. Stars burst behind his eyelids, brilliant flickers of explosions like July fourth, except without the soundtrack. The only noise in the room was his own desperate thrashing. As the starbursts gathered together and began to turn into total darkness, Travis was hauled out of the water, choking and spewing. He barely had time to clear his lungs and get a breath before he was pushed under again.

This time his brain was working against him. He couldn't make himself think of anything rational, couldn't overcome the desperate need to fight for survival. It was when he gave up trying to think of something else that he thought of something else. Caleigh showed up, smiling. When she pressed her body to his, he could almost feel it. And when she started to sing, he could almost hear it. He closed his eyes and let the music wash over him, let her presence and her smile soothe and calm him. A few seconds later when the darkness came for him, he was ready. He stopped fighting, stopped thinking or feeling, and sank gratefully into oblivion with his wife by his side, holding his hand and singing a song.

* * *

CALEIGH HAD BEEN FEELING anxious since the Admiral went away. For three days, she tried to keep up with her routine like nothing was wrong. Outwardly nothing was wrong. There was nothing in the news about a cataclysmic military situation, nothing about a four star admiral being secreted away to try and save the world. There was also no word from the Admiral. Either he had forgotten about her or he was somewhere that didn't allow communication. All Caleigh knew was that he was there one minute eating supper and gone the next. Now she was living in his too-big house alone, trying to decide what to do. She had come there to spend time with him. If he wasn't there, should she go home? Or should she stay and wait for his return? How long would it be until he came back?

On the third day, she decided to go. She finished packing her bags, set them on the floor, and felt the uncomfortable sensation she wasn't alone in the house anymore. Slowly, silently, she eased to the closet and pulled out a lacrosse stick. Raising it over her head, she stepped into the hallway and squealed, dropping the stick along with her courage.

"Sorry, I would have yelled, but I didn't know if you were home or not."

"Gage, what are you doing here?" She pressed her hand to her heart in a futile effort to stop it from trying to escape her chest. Of course she couldn't expect Gage to knock when he entered his father's house, but some warning would have been nice.

"I'm sorry. I didn't mean to startle you." He paused, looking down. "Is that a lacrosse stick?"

Caleigh laughed as she bent over to pick it up. "Yes. I guess I thought I would catch you in the net or something. I don't know. It was the only weapon that came to mind, for all the good it did me. I stink at vigilantism, apparently." She looked up with a smile that died when she saw the expression on his face. "Gage, what is it? Is it your dad? Did something happen? He left so abruptly and without word. I didn't know…" she trailed off, feeling helpless and baffled.

He reached out a hand, clasping hers. Later she would realize the hand was for support, but she didn't know if it was for her support or his. He was ashen. "It's not Dad, Caleigh. It's Travis."

* * *

"Nope, he's alive."

"He doesn't look it."

"Does he ever?"

There was only one person who would joke at a time like this. Travis peeled his eyes open and peered into the face of Kelsey Adams, hovering too close for comfort.

"Dude, your breath stinks. Word to the wise: use a mint once in a while," Kelsey whispered.

Travis blinked and even that small action hurt. Two things registered at once. The first was that he was still bound to the chair where he had been tortured. The second was that Kelsey and Truck were now beside him. His mouth worked up and down, trying to draw enough moisture to speak. "What took you so long?" he finally managed to slur.

"Truck wanted to stop for souvenirs," Kelsey said. "I told him it was all made in China, but he wouldn't believe me until he stopped and read the labels." While he talked, he worked at the bindings on Travis's arms. "This stuff's not made in China. Where'd they get Russian cuffs? Don't answer—Russia, I know."

The report of gunfire rang in the not too distant area. "Who else is here?"

"Not enough of us," Truck said. He was busy snapping pictures, stepping over a body on the floor to do so. "You about done there?" He looked over his shoulder at Kelsey.

"Houdini made this look so easy," Kelsey muttered as he tugged and sawed at the cuffs. Frustrated with the slow progress, Truck advanced, shoved Kelsey aside, pulled out a wicked-looking and unsanctioned Bowie knife, and cut the bindings. "Hey," Kelsey complained. "How come I don't have one of those?"

"Come to the party prepared or don't come at all," Truck said, shoving the knife back in its holder. They each took a side as they pulled Travis up. He didn't scream, but he wanted to. The bindings had cut his circulation, and now it rushed back with a vengeance. Later he would feel the rest of his injuries, but for now the gush of blood to his extremities was enough to focus on.

They stepped over another body as they headed outside. "I wanted to do that one," Travis complained. "He ripped out one of my molars."

"You can kill the next team who tortures you," Kelsey promised. "There's plenty enough for all of us, Greedy Gordon. You've got to learn to take turns and share, kid."

"Where's Nick?" Travis asked. He wondered if Nick was the type of leader to stay behind and command or if he would be there, up to his neck in action. Suddenly one of Travis's captors rounded a bend, his gun held high for about three seconds until his head exploded into vapor.

"He's about eight hundred yards that way," Kelsey said, nodding his head in the direction the bullet had come from.

More people were coming. They had no way of knowing if it was the good guys or the bad guys. By unspoken agreement, Kelsey took Travis, throwing him over his shoulders while Truck pulled the machine gun from his back. It was the bad guys. Truck sprayed them with bullets while Kelsey picked up the pace, running through the center of the path Truck created for them.

"Close your eyes if you get car sick, keep your hands and feet inside the vehicle until the ride is over, and don't puke down my back," Kelsey warned and then he turned his jog into a sprint.

At some point during their getaway, Travis passed out again. He was frustrated at having missed the action, but when Kelsey told him Hanlan emerged from the woods in time to save their lives, some of his frustration eased. He didn't want to see a guy he hated do a good deed for which there was no way to repay him.

With Hanlan going before, Truck bringing up the rear, and Nick watching and shooting from a distance, they made it back to camp intact, although Travis did puke down Kelsey's back—twice. Kelsey laid him on a cot before depositing his soiled shirt on the floor.

"If you weren't such a wuss about withstanding prolonged torture, I would totally make you clean that up," Kelsey said. His lip was curled in disgust, but Travis mustered a smile as Kelsey pulled off his t-shirt, too. Apparently the puke had been potent enough to soak through both layers.

"Gee, sorry," Travis muttered with no sincerity. "I guess you'll have to use those baby wipes the rest of us are supposed to pretend we don't know you carry everywhere."

The Admiral came into the tent then. He paused as his eyes scanned Travis before resting on Kelsey's shirtless form.

"It's not what it looks like, sir," Kelsey said. "*He* came on to *me.*"

Travis had to give him props for that one. Most people became so nervous they lost their sense of humor around his father. The Admiral shook his head and waved a dismissive hand toward the entrance. "As you were, Sergeant."

"Aye, sir," Kelsey said. He picked up his shirts with the tips of his fingers, grimacing as he left the tent.

"There is something seriously wrong with that boy," Caldwell said. He sank beside the bed, groaning with the effort.

"He grows on you," Travis said.

"He would have to," the Admiral said. He cleared his throat. "So, how are you?"

Travis hadn't seen a medic yet for an official diagnosis, but he could guess how bad he looked. He wasn't sure what his father wanted him to say. "Fine, I guess," he said. There was nothing time and a whole lot of pain reliever wouldn't fix, so he supposed that was true. But at this moment he was hungry, thirsty, exhausted, and sore. He didn't want to have it out with his father. He simply wanted morphine, food, and a nap—in that order.

"The medic is on base for some type of emergency. They went to retrieve him, but it's going to be about an hour. Sorry. Can I get you anything?"

"Water," Travis croaked.

"Oh, right, sorry." He scurried to the cupboard in the corner and came back with a bottle of water before awkwardly lifting Travis to a sitting position so he could help him drink. The water washed down his throat along with a whole lot of blood. He wanted to swish his mouth and spit, but he was too thirsty. He drank greedily until the bottle was gone and then fought the urge to heave again. Less than anything in the world did he feel like having his father there, but, as usual, the old man didn't seem to care about Travis's wishes.

"I thought maybe we could have a talk," Caldwell began. "And now is a good time because you seem incapable of talking back."

Was his father actually cracking a joke? If his half smile was any indication, the answer was yes. It would do no good to argue, to plead his case, to remind the Admiral that he wasn't in the mood for a lecture. Instead he sat back and prepared to let his mind drift. How much trouble would he be in if he fell asleep?

Sensing he was losing his captive audience, the Admiral dove in. "When Gage was one, your mother left me."

Travis turned his head with a wince. "No way," he blurted. His mother was the most devoted wife and mother he had ever met. No way had she taken Gage and left.

The Admiral nodded. "We lived apart for almost two years, and not because I was on assignment. That was how long it took me to grow up and realize she was the best thing that ever happened to me."

This was further proof his father wasn't quite right in the head. How could it have taken him two years to see that his wife was the most wonderful person in the world? This time when the Admiral started to talk, he had Travis's full attention.

"I was this messed up navy brat with a big head and an even bigger mouth. I thought I had all the answers. Margaret was sweet and beautiful. I thought things were okay between us, but they weren't. She tried to tell me a few times before she left, tried to talk it out, but I wasn't much into conversation back then. So she packed up her belongings and Gage and moved out. I think you'll understand when I tell you my first reaction was anger. How could she leave me when she had promised forever? She was the one who wanted to get married and start a family. I did it to make her happy. It took a really long time for the anger to burn itself off. If we hadn't had Gage as a connection, then maybe the anger would have stayed forever. But he gave me a reason to move past it.

"When I started to move past it, I started to listen to your mom, to really listen to what she was saying. She wasn't saying she didn't love me. She wasn't saying she didn't want to be married anymore. She was saying she loved me with everything she had and that my inability to love her in return was killing her. Leaving was the only way she knew to get my attention, to try and make me listen.

"You're going to find this hard to believe, but I have a really hard head. And I also have a tendency to always think I'm right. But almost losing your mom and Gage broke through those barriers. I changed, Trav. I changed for them. I started studying the men around me that I admired and trying to emulate them. Before that I had only had my dad's poor example. I wasn't like him, so I thought I was doing okay, but I wasn't.

"I became the kind of husband your mom deserved. I listened to her, I spent time with her. I loved her, and I told her so. From then on, we had a good marriage. I haven't been a perfect father, but I was a good husband. What your mom and I had was so special I haven't even tried to duplicate it with someone else. How could I?"

Travis's mouth hurt too much to respond, but he couldn't have if he wanted to. This was the closest he had ever heard his father sound to human, and he was stunned. The Admiral continued. Travis stared at him in rapt fascination.

"The last couple of weeks have made me think about a lot of things, specifically you and I. I never realized before how much alike we are."

Travis made a choking sound. The Admiral laughed.

"You think about it and get over the shock, and you'll realize it's true. This new realization has made me understand everything I've tried to do for you was to save you from the same mistakes I made. I went about it wrong, but my intentions were good. There's nothing I can do to make you come around to my way of thinking anymore. You're a grown man. So all I can do is give you some advice and hope you'll take it. Caleigh is your Margaret, son. People like us, people with hard heads and big mouths who are bent on self-destruction, don't get many chances with people like them, people who are genuinely good and kind and make life better by being alive. This is your chance. Don't blow it. Do what you have to in order to make it work with her." He stood and headed to the door, not waiting for a reply. When he reached the flap of the tent he paused. "I'm proud of you," he said. His words were clear and strong, even if he didn't turn in Travis's direction. Then he pushed aside the flap and walked away.

CHAPTER 18

"Do you want me to go with you?"

Gage hadn't left Caleigh's side since imparting the news of Travis's capture and subsequent rescue. She was especially thankful for his presence as they flew over the ocean to Landstuhl Hospital in Germany. Caleigh had never left the country before. Even though everyone at the hospital spoke English, she was overwhelmed and insecure. Gage took everything in stride, putting her at ease by telling her how many times he had landed at the hospital as a patient while he was a SEAL. Now they were finally able to see Travis, and Caleigh was nervous all over again.

"Why don't you go first?" she suggested. If Gage went first, he would be able to prepare her if Travis was injured more than they thought he was. Details of his injuries had been sketchy. A convoy in Turkey had an accident with mass casualties and the hospital was aflutter with activity as they awaited the newest rush of patients. Seemingly no one had time to talk to her about her husband.

As she watched Gage walk away, her anxiety inched up another notch.

"Hey, little girl. Want some candy?"

145

Caleigh looked up to see Kelsey looming over her. She burst into tears.

"That's not the effect I usually have on women," he said. He sat and pulled her into a hug. She cried on his shoulder for a couple of minutes.

"Your shirt smells like puke," she murmured, though she didn't pull away.

"Thank your husband for that. As soon as I get stateside, I'm burning it."

"How is he really?" she asked. "Everyone is so cagey about his condition."

"He's fine, sort of a sissy, really. He tries to pretend he's all tough, but I can tell by his stoic expression and lack of complaining he's enjoying the attention."

She laughed and wiped her eyes. "Thanks for everything. They didn't give me a lot of details, but I know you were part of his rescue."

"I sort of owed you one," he said.

"Lolly's death wasn't your fault," she said.

"That's what I tell myself every morning," he said. "Someday I'm going to believe it. What was between you guys anyway? Every time I tried to ask him, he blushed and stammered like a little girl."

"That was basically what was between us—a lot of blushing, a lot of stammering, and feelings as pure as the driven snow. I don't know if anything would have come of us or not. In some ways I think we were too alike."

"You mean you were both angelically good," he said.

"Yeah, I guess I sort of do mean that. I like having someone a little bit bad. Is that crazy?"

"Yes, but you're a woman, so it's allowed. I'll tell you a little secret —I purposely misuse a woman's name in order to show them I'm a shallow jerk, and they eat it up. Why do women like being mistreated? I don't get it."

"Melly doesn't," Caleigh said, shooting him a surreptitious glance.

"No, Melly definitely does not allow herself to be mistreated. But I think we know Melly's the exception to every rule."

"You say that like a bad thing."

"It's good because it makes Melly who she is, but it's bad because it makes her not mine," he explained.

"Kelsey, you're being obtuse. Don't let the best thing that's ever happened to you get away because of misplaced pride. Marry the woman and give her a baby. Otherwise, you're going to be the godfather at her baby's christening." She nodded in the direction of Gage who was advancing on them from the direction of Travis's room.

His hand tensed on your forearm. "Why? What do you know? What's going on between them? How serious are they?"

Her answer was in the form of a knowing little smile. "Sorry. I only share secrets with someone who has the guts to go after what he really wants."

"I'm cutting off access to my dog. Get your own," he called to her retreating backside. She laughed and threw a wave over her shoulder. Gage sat a couple of chairs away from Kelsey and stared at the opposing wall. They sat in awkward silence until Kelsey couldn't take it anymore.

"Yeah, I'm going to need you to stay away from Melly," he said.

Gage turned to look at him, one eyebrow raised in question. "I'm going to need a compelling reason."

"She's mine."

"I wasn't aware she was a possession," Gage said.

"Now you know. She's mine, she's off limits, the end."

"Does she know? Because she hasn't mentioned you since you've been gone," Gage said.

"That's how you know she really cares. The more she opens up and talks about something, the less it mean to her. She talks about you a lot. All the time, really." It was a lie, but Gage didn't need to know that.

He sat back and crossed his arms, regarding Kelsey with a calculating gaze. "Here's the thing: I don't encroach on another guy's territory. It's not my thing. But as far as I can tell, Melly's not your territory. To quote Beyoncé, if you like it, you'd better put a ring on it."

"First of all, Beyoncé? I lost any respect I once had for you. Second,

I don't need a ring to know how I feel about her or how she feels about me."

"Yes, but she does," Gage pointed out.

"It's inevitable that Melly and I are going to end up together. It's the way it is, so back off," Kelsey said. His irritation was growing beyond what his rational mind could handle.

"If it's inevitable, why not make it official now? What are you waiting for?"

"What are you, the marriage police?" Kelsey asked. "And why are you trying to get me to propose to your girlfriend?"

"Oh, she's not my girlfriend. Did I forget to mention we broke up? Not enough chemistry. She's a good friend, though. Nice girl, Melly." He stood and slapped Kelsey on the leg. "I'm going for coffee. You want anything?"

"To forget the last fifteen minutes of my life, especially the part about Beyoncé."

Gage gave him a heads up nod and left smiling, secure in the knowledge that he had won another round. "Man, I hate that guy," Kelsey muttered. He wasn't accustomed to losing verbal sparring matches, yet Gage had bested him twice. He didn't really hate him, though. As long as he wasn't dating Melly, he felt a sort of begrudging acceptance and admiration for the loser. "Stupid sailors," he added before his positive thoughts could make him forget Gage was a navy man.

DOWN THE HALL, Caleigh paused outside Travis's room and took a breath to prepare herself for whatever she might face. The Admiral had said Travis's mother was the perfect military wife, and that was a lot to live up to. Caleigh was an emotional creature. Holding back her feelings and reactions didn't come naturally to her, but she would do it if that was what military wives were supposed to do. After one more reassuring breath, she stepped through the door.

Travis's hands were bandaged, and so was his chest. His eyes were swollen and purple, his nose broken and disjointed, and his lips split. There were burns, cuts, and bruises all over his body and patches where the hair had been torn from his head. He looked like someone who had been in a bad car accident; she couldn't wrap her mind around the fact that human beings had done this to him. She wanted to burst into noisy tears, run to him, and curl up beside him for reassurance. Instead she walked sedately into the room.

Travis saw her enter the room and his heart sank. She was beautiful, but her subdued reaction revealed the truth—she was no longer his. The letter she had sent had been a goodbye. How else to explain her coolness and reserve? They hadn't seen each other for six months, he had been tortured and left for dead, and this was her greeting?

"Hi," she said.

"Hi," he said. The word came out sharper than he intended and she flinched.

"I'm sorry about this," she said. She gestured toward the bed and looked away, staring at the opposing wall.

He wasn't sure how to respond to that. Was she sorry he was injured, or sorry she was breaking up with him while he was down? He wanted to tell her to say what she needed to say and get out, to make the first strike and keep the upper hand. He opened his mouth to do it and stopped. He didn't want her to go. He wanted her to stay; he wanted her to be the way she had been before he went away. Unbidden, the Admiral's words echoed in his head. For the first time, Travis found himself searching his mind for every piece of advice his father had given him on marriage. "How are you doing?" he asked.

Her lower lip quivered and her eyes filled with tears. "I want so much to be a grownup, to be a good military wife who doesn't fall apart when things like this happen, but I don't think it's working."

He blinked at her in confusion. What was she saying? Was she trying to tell him she was upset and trying to hold it in? His heart kicked up the pace and he grimaced. The electric shocks had left some damage behind. "Babygirl, it's okay. You can cry. I won't tell the other military wives."

Tears began streaming unchecked down her cheeks. "Oh, Travis," she said. Her voice wobbled and his heart turned over again. She cared. He opened his arms and she stumbled forward, momentarily forgetting his broken ribs. His breath left in a rush when she pressed up against him, but he didn't care. He was holding her, and he never wanted to let her go. His only regret was that his hands were taped and he couldn't feel her skin under his fingertips.

"I was so afraid." She whispered the words as if admitting a shameful secret, but Travis was heartened. She couldn't want out of the marriage if she felt this way, could she? She trembled with renewed fear as she wept. Travis held her and soothed her, feeling better than he had in months. Then his hand smoothed over her flat stomach and they froze. She hadn't told him about the baby. He was still angry about that. The feelings of resentment and hurt rushed back at him. He wanted to accuse, to rail, to defend his heart from pain and vulnerability. But something held him back again.

"You lost the baby," he said. He tried to keep his tone neutral to invite a response other than anger and defensiveness on her part. She didn't reply, though. She nodded and cried harder.

"He was so beautiful," she choked. "He looked like you."

Tears slammed behind his eyelids and lingered. "Why didn't you tell me?" he managed a croaky whisper.

"Because I didn't think you would care, and I couldn't stand it if you didn't." She pulled away and looked at him. "That was selfish, and I'm sorry. But I wasn't thinking clearly at the time." Her hand smoothed over the undamaged part of his cheek.

"Caleigh, you've got to learn to fight better. If you accuse yourself and apologize, then there's nothing left for me to do."

She smiled and sniffled. "I'll work on it," she said.

They stared at each other in silence a few minutes, letting the intimacy from their early marriage wash over them and descend. "I'm sorry about…about the baby," Travis said. He cleared his throat and looked down. "I said stuff and acted like a jerk, but I didn't mean it. I was looking forward to being a dad." He hadn't cried since he was fourteen, since his dad took him under his wing and told him it was time to be a man. Tears choked his throat, cutting off his air, but he still wouldn't give in to them. Instead he cleared his throat again and looked down at Caleigh's hands.

"Travis, we can't go on like we were before," Caleigh said. His head snapped up as his tears disappeared, only to be replaced by anger. So she was dumping him. Great. Way to kick a guy when he was down.

"I think I owe you an apology," Caleigh said. Travis was only half listening while he prepared a defense. If she thought he was going to make this easy, then she was mistaken. "I said I loved you when we were married, but I don't think I did."

He winced. Apparently Caleigh did know how to wound in a fight. His breathing became hitched with pain. He wanted to click the meter on his pain pump to administer another hit, but he decided to wait. Better to take his blows while he had a clear head and could remember them.

"I think I loved the idea of you," Caleigh continued. "I loved who I wanted you to be. But I didn't love *you*. How could I? I didn't even know you. That was my fault. I was living in fantasy land. Then after the baby things were so dark. I wanted out. Gage came and brought me your old scrapbooks. I started looking through them, more because I told him I would than because I actually wanted to. But something magical happened. I think I actually started to fall in love with you."

His mind drifted back from the place he had sent it for safekeeping. "What?" he blurted.

She smiled and smoothed her fingers over his cheek again. "You were an awkward kid, no doubt about that. But there was something in your eyes that tugged at my heart."

"Dorkiness?" he guessed.

"And loneliness and courage and stubbornness and strength and everything else I've come to understand about you. After I finished with the scrapbooks, I went to visit your Aunt Holly."

"You visited Holly?" he said.

"Yes. We hit it off really well, by the way. She was happy to tell me lots of stories about you. Trouble maker." She reached to poke his ribs, thought better of it, and dropped her hand. "I was starting to get a clearer picture of who you are, but there were still gaps. So I moved in with your dad."

She said the last part while he was taking a sip of water. He choked, spewing water over both of them, and then had a coughing session that left him shaking and gasping for breath.

"I'm sorry," Caleigh said over and over as she attempted to sop up the spilled water. "I didn't think that would come as such a surprise."

"You moved in with the Admiral?" he said as soon as he could draw a breath. He couldn't fathom that anyone had willingly moved in with his father when he hadn't been able to wait until he could get away. "For me?" he added.

"In the beginning," she said. "I wanted to know you, to really know you. It became like a quest. But along the way I got to know myself. This is going to sound dumb, but I never had any aspirations other than being a wife and mom. I never saw myself as being good at anything or capable of anything. But I knew I was caring and compassionate, I would be good at being a wife and mom. Then I lost the baby and we were having problems. Suddenly all my dreams were in ashes. I started volunteering at the VA, working with kids whose parents were deployed. I did it because I wanted to know what it was like for you, growing up while your dad was away so much of the time. But it ended up being for me. At your dad's, I was Caleigh. Not Ashleigh's little sister or Pastor Desmond's daughter, or even Travis's wife. Just me. And I found out I like me." Her eyes fell to his chest. "And I like you, too."

"You like me?" he said. She nodded. "Why?" he blurted. "Caleigh, I'm a jerk. You could do so much better than me."

She looked at him then, and she was angry. "Don't say that. Don't sell yourself short. We're young and immature, we have issues, but we have potential."

It was beyond kind of her to lump herself in with him. He was immature, he was the one with issues. As for potential…

"Caleigh, this is who I am. I say the wrong thing. I make terrible decisions. I hurt those around me."

"I know," she said. "But you're also strong. You're so strong, Travis.

You have to understand I've been a people pleaser my whole life. I do what other people want because I don't want to upset them or rock the boat. But sometimes I'm so tired of never being who I am or doing what I want. I'm always who everyone else wants me to be, I always do what everyone else wants me to do. You're always you. You always do what you want. Both extremes are bad. Don't you think we could both sort of move toward the center? Maybe I could teach you how to bend and you could teach me how not to bend? Maybe we could meet somewhere in the middle." She bit her lip and searched for another uninjured spot to touch. Finding none, she settled for his cheek again. "I can't go back to the way it was. I want to be with you, I want to stay married to you, but I want to be happy. I want to be in a marriage that works. I don't want to hurt anymore."

"I don't know if I can do it, but I'm willing to try," he said.

Her eyes lit with hope, the same hope he was feeling in his heart. "There's one thing, one deal breaker we have to agree on. No other women. No Vegas strip shows, nothing of that sort. That's the one area I'm not willing to compromise. I will not share my man."

She sounded so vehement a part of him wanted to smile. The other part wanted to rebel. He had never been good with restrictions or ultimatums. For a few minutes, he waged an inner battle. He didn't want to give up, but he realized it wasn't the other women or Vegas he was fighting for; it was his independence. And, really, he could let it go. He didn't care about the other women. He cared about Caleigh, and it was time he showed her. "I swear to you I will never go to another show like that again."

Caleigh smiled. "See? This is where you being a strong man of your word comes in handy because I believe you. I trust you. If you say it, then I know you mean it and I won't have to worry about this again."

"Caleigh, you make losing feel like winning," he said. "And I love you."

Her eyes filled with tears and overflowed again. She dashed the moisture away. "Drat it all, I'll never make it as a military wife if these tears keep up."

"I don't care if you're not a military wife. You're my wife, and I intend to keep you that way."

"How painful would it be if I kiss you?" she asked.

"Not as painful as if you don't," he said. He pulled her closer and kissed her, with far more gentleness and restraint than he wanted. By the time the kiss ended, he had rallied his courage to say what he had wanted to say for months, the thing he'd been practicing in his head and wasn't sure he'd ever have the guts to admit. "I don't want to lose you. I don't want to lose our marriage. You took me by surprise. So much that I think my predominant emotion these last few months has been shock. I didn't expect to love you, didn't expect to love being married to you. Honestly I thought we'd stay together until we couldn't take it anymore and then split up. But I love you. No, I freaking *adore* you, and I love being married to you. I love our little life together in our cozy little house. I love waking up to you each morning, coming home to you each evening, and going to bed with you each night. I want to be with you. But it's not going to be easy. You know what I'm like. I'm going to do my best, Caleigh. But I can't promise it's going to be easy."

"Who said it needs to be easy?" Caleigh asked, affronted. "We're part of the marines; it's our job to do everything the hard way. Besides, maybe you're a big grump, but I hear your wife is a real sweetheart. Maybe she'll balance you out."

"My wife *is* a sweetheart," he said. "With the patience and temperament of a saint. And it's time I started to appreciate her." It was painful, but he kissed her again before urging her to climb in beside him. It was excruciating, but he managed to get his arms fully around her while she rested her head on his chest. His bandaged hand stroked over her hair. "This was what I pictured when they were doing their best to kill me," Travis whispered. "I tried thinking of anything else, but you were the only thing that stuck, the only thing that saw me through. And you were singing. I love it when you sing."

"I thought you hated it," Caleigh said.

"Only when it makes me miss the final score of the World Series," he said. "Maybe you could sing during commercials."

"When you're better, I'm going to make you pay for that remark."

"I'll hold you to it," Travis said.

"As long as you hold me, I don't care why," Caleigh said. It was probably going to kill him, but she snuggled closer, trying to be as gentle as possible as she pressed her face to his neck and breathed in. His scent was familiar somehow, like coming home. "I love you," she said. "For real this time." There was no reply. When she opened her eyes and looked up, he was fast asleep. They had come a long way, Caleigh thought. Travis had learned marriage could have good times while she had realized marriage could have bad times, and both were okay. The ups and downs were what made a relationship real. She understood now that marriage wasn't the fun fantasy she had always dreamed, and it wasn't as easy as her parents and sister made it look. It was hard work. She and Travis undoubtedly had a difficult road ahead, but somehow she knew they would make it. With her optimism and his tenacity, they could survive anything. She chuckled to herself as she realized she had an ace in the hole. From now on when times got tough, Caleigh would remind Travis that if he had survived torture at the hands of enemy combatants, he could survive marriage to her. And maybe because she was able to look on the bright side she would make it as a military wife after all.

Finally secure in the knowledge that she loved and was loved in return, Caleigh closed her eyes and fell asleep.

CHAPTER 19

Kelsey poked his head in the door after a few minutes of prolonged silence. He had shamelessly eavesdropped on the pretense of making sure Caleigh was okay. The truth was he was nosy about how their reunion would go down. He was surprised by how well it went and by how grownup both of them sounded. When had that happened? How had two of the most immature people he knew suddenly turned into responsible adults? What changed them?

Marriage.

"Shut up," Kelsey whispered. The voice in his head, the one that passed for his version of a conscience, had started to sound a whole lot like Lolly lately. When the little guy had been alive, Kelsey had called him Jiminy Cricket because of his never-ending attempts to steer the team in the right direction. Somehow it had worked. Too bad Lolly hadn't survived to see the outcome of all his hard work. Nick was happily married and a commanding officer. Truck had slain his inner demons and was on his way to becoming an ace family man. Even the new guy was turning out all right. And Kelsey, well, at least he wasn't crazy anymore. That was something.

I beg to differ.

Kelsey wasn't too surprised to see Lolly sitting beside him. He had been functioning on no sleep and too much adrenaline since Travis was taken hostage. Maybe if he ignored it, the illusion would go away.

Good luck with that.

"What do you want?" Kelsey asked. He glanced around the hallway to make sure no one saw him talking to himself. He was alone. Except for the mirage of his dead friend.

I want to talk. Why are you so jumpy?

"Uh, because you're dead, and if I'm seeing you then either I'm dead or I'm still crazy. I've reached the limit of my deductible, so I hope it's not the crazy making an encore appearance."

Lolly laughed. *Man, you kill me.*

"Great, the dead guy is making jokes. Everyone's a comedian."

Lolly laughed again and shook his head. *Seriously, though, what's up with you and Melly, Jaws?*

"Don't you know? I thought ghosts knew everything."

Don't confuse death with omniscience.

"See, now you're starting to freak me out because I don't even know what that word means. If you're imaginary, how did I come up with that?"

Lolly smiled, waiting him out. Kelsey sighed. "I'm taking care of her like I promised."

Lolly didn't say a word. Instead he sat patiently, the smile still pasted on his face.

"It's probably better that I do it from a distance anyway," Kelsey added. He had never been able to stand silence, even if it was created by his own imagination. "I mean, I'm nobody's idea of husband material. Can you imagine me married? With kids?" He tried to picture it, and the image came too easily. He doubled over and pressed his fists to his eyes. "Uh-oh."

Lolly laughed hard. Kelsey looked up to scowl at him, but he was gone. His laughter remained for a long time, though, echoing loudly in Kelsey's head.

* * *

Melly was waiting for him at the docks. She stood on the pier with Rocky beside her. At least Kelsey thought it was Rocky. From a distance it looked like a harlequin grizzly bear. The dog had finally grown into his feet. Now in a sitting position his head was almost even with Melly's shoulder.

Kelsey stepped off the plank and walked purposefully in her direction. Rocky whimpered and squirmed, but didn't stand up. Melly had been taking him to obedience school, and it appeared to be working. He dropped his bags and started to reach for her, but she held him off.

"Wait, I have something to show you. I taught Rocky a trick. Daddy's home, Rocky. Salute."

The dog raised one gigantic paw to his eyes as if shielding them from the sun. Kelsey smiled at the dog and dropped to his knees in front of Melly. "I lose; you win. Marry me."

"Because I taught the dog to salute?" she asked. She sounded baffled.

"No, because you're everything and I can't take it anymore." He scooted forward and pressed his face to her stomach.

She rested her hands on his shoulders, leaned down and kissed the top of his head. "No."

He craned his neck to look up at her. "What?"

"No. I can't marry you."

He scooted back so he didn't have to bend his neck so far. "I asked you out and you said you wanted commitment. I asked you to move in with me and you said you wanted marriage. I asked you to marry me, and you said no. What do you want, Melly? Please, put me out of my misery and explain it because you're killing me."

"I'll tell you what I don't want. I don't want to have to drag someone to the altar kicking and screaming for his lost independence. I don't want to spend the rest of my life with someone who resents me for tying him down. I don't want someone who feels like he's losing by marrying me."

She sounded so miffed he laughed and shook his head in exasperation. "I swear, Melly, only you could get angry at a marriage proposal. You can't ever make anything easy for me, can you? Fine, here goes. It took six months in the wilderness with twenty-nine other men for me to come to the conclusion *I'm* Tiny Tim Stokes. I have no one if I don't have you. And the death knell for my so-called independence came when I realized I was jealous of Travis. Travis, Melly. You made me jealous of a mixed up stupid kid with ten broken fingers because he and Caleigh have something we don't. So maybe you're right, maybe marriage changes things, and maybe I want it now. And maybe you're winning the battle, but I'm winning the war because I'm getting you. And that's all I want, Melly. You're all I want. I'm tired of pretending there's something else out there when I know there isn't. You're the end of my road and the end of my rainbow. You're my pot of gold."

"Ask again," she whispered. Tears shimmered on her lashes and her lower lip quivered.

"What was that? I couldn't quite hear you," he said.

She jabbed him in the side of the neck. "I said ask again, you miserable heathen."

He gave a longsuffering sigh. "Okay." This time he remembered the ring he had purchased before leaving Germany. He pulled the box from his pocket and held it out to her. "Melly, would you pretty please marry me? And if you don't say yes, I swear you will rue the day you were born, woman."

"I'd be delighted," Melly said.

Kelsey removed the ring from its container and slipped it on her finger. "Duly noted you couldn't quite manage a yes," he said.

"I wouldn't want you to get the idea I'm suddenly going to be obedient because we're getting married."

"I wouldn't dream of making that mistake." He stood and pulled her into his arms. "Don't you dare kiss me."

"Now you're learning," Melly said, then she stood on her toes and kissed him until Rocky started to howl in protest of being ignored too long.

EPILOGUE

The team didn't stay together for as long as any of them wanted. Truck and Shelby were the first to go—shipped off to Camp Pendleton in California soon after they were married, they began their dream of fostering children. They adopted two of their foster kids before having another two biologically. Even though they made their home in California for many years, they never lost touch with their east coast family, and when Truck retired from the marines they moved back.

Travis was the next to go. Kelsey was the one who pointed out that his thick skin and inability to take an insult to heart would make for a perfect drill sergeant. As soon as he met the qualifications, he and Caleigh moved to Parris Island where he helped train new recruits. They had a girl and a boy after Caleigh finished her degree. She became a CPA and managed other people's money until she had children, and then she became a financial counselor, working from home.

Nick worked his way through the ranks until he wound up in Washington. No one was quite sure how it happened, no one but Nick who understood that a certain Admiral had been paving the path for him. By the time he retired, he was a brigadier general at the Pentagon. He and Ashleigh had four sons. One followed in his father's footsteps and became an officer in the marines. The other three followed in their mother's footsteps and opened a construction company. She taught them everything she knew.

Kelsey also transitioned to teaching new recruits. He went back to sniper school and took great pleasure in making sure subsequent batches of shooters and spotters were perfect. He eventually earned the rank of sergeant major and was the only one of the team to stay at Camp Lejeune for the remainder of his career. He and Melly had three daughters. Much to his chagrin, his charms were as useless on them as they were on their mother. Melly liked to say it was because God knew she would need help keeping him in line. Four women could accomplish more than one. Kelsey liked to say it was because God knew he had too much love for one woman. Four seemed like enough. His daughters took delight in dressing him in their frilliest pink boas and hats for tea parties, and he grudgingly went along. When they got a little older, they pooled their money and bought him a shirt that read "World's Best Dad." From then on, he never complained about the boas or hats again.

THANK you for reading the *Point Man,* the final book in the Brothers Courageous series. For more books, please check out my website at www.vanessagraybartal.com

9 781953 339096